Miss Hewitt Investigates the White Cat

Linda Stephenson

Miss Hewitt Investigates the White Cat

Jasper Rabbit Books

About the author.

Linda Stephenson has been a professional writer since 1981, working mainly in the juvenile comics market. As well as eBooks, she has also published plays at <u>www.lazybeescripts.co.uk</u> and non-fiction books on circus skills and magic. One play, Bradley No Mates, won a drama festival with a youth group from Liverpool. She presents a radio show on a local station and writes all her own stories and material. She is married and lives in Bedfordshire.

Miss Hewitt Investigates the White Cat

This is a work of fiction. The characters, situations and places, except for those already in the public domain, are products of the author's imagination. Any similarity between them and any person living or dead is entirely a coincidence.

The author has exerted the right to be identified as the author of this work in accordance with the Copyrights, Designs and Patents Act 1988.

This book is copyright. No reproduction without permission from the publishers.

In memory of Eva Thurley

1916-2014

© *2014 Linda Stephenson*

The Miss Hewitt series also available as kindle eBooks:

Miss Hewitt's Case Book

*Miss Hewitt Investigates the Return of the Ripper.

*Miss Hewitt Investigates the Man in the Tree.

*Miss Hewitt Investigates the Suicide.

*Also available as print books.

Audio books narrated by Julia Eve (www.juliaeve.com)

Miss Hewitt Investigates

Miss Hewitt Investigates the Suffragette

Miss Hewitt Investigates the Medium

Miss Hewitt Investigates the Children's Home.

Also by Linda Stephenson as kindle eBooks:

The Waterloo Man.

Flowers in the Afternoon.

Popple Beach

The Black Spot

Islington

Pretty Boy Guthrie

Foreword

London, Spring 1916.

Great Britain is at war with Germany. On the Home Front, life is becoming more dangerous as Zeppelin air raids are frequent on the mainland. The conscription of single men into the army has been introduced in January. Miss Isabel Hewitt is a lady of independent means who also works as a private detective. Born in India she is the daughter of a Captain in the Dragoons, lives in Bloomsbury and owns a lively pug named Pastry. She is assisted in her work by her maid Hattie Peach, her former manservant Clarke and, occasionally, by the pug.

CHAPTER ONE

Cartwright Gardens London Spring 1916

Lady detective Miss Isabel Hewitt slowly opened her eyes. Everywhere was dark. There was a roaring sound in her ears and something lay heavy on her chest. It was cold. She shivered. Then she remembered the air raid. Had they been bombed? They had taken shelter in the cellar when the maroons sounded. Had it afforded them sufficient protection? Was she lying in the debris of her own house? She felt she couldn't move. And she couldn't remember the all clear sounding. Her neck was stiff. Had she been knocked out? Britain was still at war with Germany and Zeppelin raids continued on the mainland, adding terror on the Home Front. The war was not going well, but a new offensive was being planned by General Haig on the 12 mile stretch along the River Somme in France. The allies wanted to protect the French town of Verdun. The army had suffered severe losses and could no longer rely on volunteers. The conscription of single men had been introduced in January.

She had no idea of the time. Where were Clarke, her former manservant and beloved confidant, Hattie her maid, and Pastry her pet pug? Were they safe or dead? She tried to move, but her whole body ached. What was pressing down on her chest? Suddenly a light flashed before her eyes. Someone had turned on a light. She started, blinked and saw Hattie, in a dressing gown, walking down the cellar steps with a tray of tea and biscuits. The something moved on her chest and jumped off. It was Pastry, who had also been snoring in her ear and now sensed food was on its way.

"You're awake, Ma'am," said Hattie smiling and walking across the cellar floor. "You were sound off earlier, Mr Clarke said not to trouble you."

Isabel, breathing a sigh of relief, pulled herself into a sitting position.

"What time is it?"

Hattie handed her a cup of tea. Isabel took it thankfully.

"7'clock, Ma'am. Mr Clarke has had breakfast. He's going to see what he can do. They copped it near Russell Square. There might be a lot of casualties he said."

Isabel took a sip of tea. Her mouth was dry. She recalled the terror of the night.

"The bombs sounded so loud. Is there any damage to the house?"

"None, Ma'am." Hattie sat on another mattress beside her. Pastry jumped up with her, eyes fixed on the biscuits. "It was a stray bomb. It just missed us."

Yes, this time thought Isabel. She glanced round the cellar with the three mattresses, blankets and pillows on the floor. How many more nights would they spend like this? But at least it would afford them some protection. For that they were fortunate, not like many residents of London and elsewhere, who were caught out if they didn't reach any shelter, or the safety of a London Underground station. She took a biscuit from the plate and instantly became the object of Pastry's imploring eyes. The pug jumped onto the cellar floor and then broke wind.

"I'll take her up to the yard," said Hattie at once. "She has been out once."

Isabel laughed. She could always rely on Pastry to lighten the mood. When the rotund little fawn pug wasn't snoring in her basket, she was playing enthusiastically with a piece of knotted rope, barking at the vacuum cleaner or, more often than not, barking at nothing at all.

"I'll do it," replied Isabel as she finished her tea. She picked up the dog and gave her the last corner of her biscuit. "It's time I went upstairs. I'd like to see Clarke before he leaves."

Clarke was currently in the Royal Medical Core. A very serious ankle injury the year before had almost healed and, once again, he was facing a medical board to assess his fitness to return to that theatre of danger they called the Western Front. He wore the blue uniform of an injured soldier and currently worked as an orderly at a small local military hospital. He still lived with her in Cartwright Gardens and was able to advise Isabel about her investigations. Much of his self-confidence had returned and he cut his former handsome figure. Hattie was secretly smitten with him, or she thought it was secret. Isabel had suspected the partiality from very early on. But Hattie was too devoted to her young, stylish mistress to do no more than cast the odd look at him. Clarke was Isabel's man and she would have been his wife had he not already been married to a brassy barmaid named Bessie, who had appeared, after an absence of many years, when war broke out, in case there was a pension in the event of his death. Isabel found such callous superficiality quite nauseating, but there was nothing she could do. She and Hattie also contributed to the war effort as members of the Women's Emergency Corps. They both drove ambulances for the same local military hospital, Isabel fitting this in with any other work she had.

Isabel carried Pastry out of the cellar, but Clarke had already left. By 9am she had washed, dressed and breakfasted, so decided to walk the pug in the gardens opposite her house, as she felt the need for some fresh air after the awkward night's sleep. Her shift as a driver did not start until the afternoon. It was a beautiful spring morning, but the air was fused with the smell of dust and fumes from the fire bomb. It had been a bit too close for comfort. Pastry meandered along, as if without a care in the world. Isabel, too, was lost in her thoughts and then, quite suddenly, the pug started barking at a rose bush.

"Pastry, there's nothing there," scolded Isabel, but the pug would not give up and became quite excited, refusing to walk on past. Then a white cat slinked out from behind the bush. Pastry barked more. The cat looked at the pug with a casual air of disdain in its blue eyes, and then set off long the path, leaving Pastry straining on her lead to get after it.

"You have seen that cat before," chuckled Isabel, but that made no difference. She was obliged to let Pastry pull her along the path until the cat elegantly leaped over the railings and disappeared down towards Tavistock Place. She wondered who owned it. It looked a valuable cat, not one she would care to let roam too far in these chancy times. Pastry continued to bark for the remainder of the walk. Back home she still seemed excited. Isabel blamed the air raid for disturbing her equilibrium. She decided to run off some of the pug's energy by playing a game of tug with the knotted rope. But, when she threw it across the room, the pug set off on what Isabel called one of her manic pug runs, tearing round and round the furniture with eyes bulging and ears back. She worked up quite a speed and was difficult to catch. Isabel was still trying to ambush her, crouching down on the floor, when the sitting room door opened and Hattie ushered two visitors inside. Isabel looked up; Pastry collided with her and knocked her backwards onto the carpet. Hattie immediately stepped forward and scooped the dog into her ample arms. The maid was a big woman, who had been brought up on a farm. She had black hair, a ruddy complexion and always wore the uniform of the Women's Emergency Corps, even though she was not due to start her shift, like Isabel, until the afternoon.

"That's enough from you," she said sternly. Pastry's little ears immediately flattened as they always did when chastised.

Isabel scrambled to her feet.

"My apologies, ladies," she said, colouring with embarrassment.

"This is Miss Howard and Miss Dunstan," announced Hattie.

"Miss Howard, Miss Dunstan, good morning," continued Isabel, straightening her skirt. "Would you care to sit down? You must excuse my dog. I think the air raid last night has upset her. Hattie, take her downstairs."

She hastily picked up the rope before either of her visitors tripped over it.

Miss Howard was an attractive, dark haired, pale young woman, dressed in smart, jet black mourning clothes. She smiled.

"I'm sure it has, Miss Hewitt. It was very close to here. I live in Russell Square. I was fortunate not to have my house damaged. Do not punish the dog on my account. She's a cutie. Please let her stay."

"Very well." Isabel looked at Hattie. "Would you bring us coffee, please, and Pastry can remain here."

The pug wriggled free and jumped onto the floor as the two visitors sat in Isabel's wing chairs and Miss Hewitt took a seat on the chesterfield. Hattie left to attend to the coffee. Miss Howard's companion, Miss Dunstan, was a much plainer woman of similar age, also dressed in black. Her manner was more severe and Isabel guessed she had a lesser sense of humour than her friend. This was born out when Pastry sniffed both ladies and became quite excited around Miss Dunstan's legs. The woman looked very defensive.

"I'm afraid I'm not very confident with dogs," she explained, trying to shoo Pastry away. "I was badly bitten as a child."

"I'm sorry," said Isabel, although the pug's tiny jaws would have difficulty making any impression on the woman's heavy, black skirt. She grabbed hold of Pastry and put her on the chesterfield beside her. "Now, how can I help?"

Miss Howard's manner instantly sobered.

"You have been recommended to me by our mutual friend, Eleanor Graves. I am in desperate need of your help." She looked at her friend. "Isn't that so Margaret?"

"Yes," agreed Miss Dunstan. She looked at Isabel. "You may have read about the savage murder of Giles Chichester?"

"Indeed I have," replied Isabel, recalling the report of how the raffish, young journalist was found stabbed to death a fortnight ago, in his fashionable apartment in Stanhope Street near Sussex Square.

"He was Jen-Eva's fiancé," continued Miss Dunstan, nodding to her friend.

"And I need you to find out who did this dreadful thing," added Miss Howard, tears suddenly welling in her eyes. She hastily pulled a lace bordered handkerchief from her sleeve. Her friend leaned forward and grabbed her hand in a gesture of comfort.

Isabel nodded.

"Have the police not been able to help, Miss Howard?"

"The Police!" The woman was dismissive, immediately regaining her composure. "And please call me Jen-Eva." She gave a sheepish smile. "I was born in Switzerland and my father named me after the city of my birth. My first name is actually Jennifer, but I have always been known as Jen-Eva."

Isabel nodded.

"Is it Inspector Mangle in charge of the case?"

"No, he is too busy elsewhere," replied Miss Dunstan releasing her hand. "A Sergeant Perch is investigating."

Isabel considered.

"The name isn't familiar. I don't think I have met him."

"You are not missing anything, Miss Hewitt," added Jen-Eva, dabbing her eyes. "The man is pompous and patronising, taking great pains to advise us that he is from a long line of police officers and we are fortunate to have him. One of his forebears was a Bow Street Runner."

"A Bow Street Runner," echoed Margaret Dunstan sarcastically.

"Indeed?" Isabel tried not to smile. She hoped the Sergeant's policing skills had improved from those of his ancestors, although he was obviously proud of his roots. She looked at Miss Howard. "I take it he has not been able to find out the identity of the killer."

Jen-Eva frowned.

"No. We have helped all we can, but so far he has discovered absolutely nothing. My darling Giles deserves justice. His killer has to be caught. I am hoping you will be more successful, Miss Hewitt."

"Very well, then begin by telling me everything you know," said Isabel. "Then I can decide whether I can help. But, I must warn you, I drive an ambulance for a local military hospital at least 3 days a week, so any investigation must be managed around my duties."

"Of course," agreed Jen-Eva. "The war comes first."

Both ladies worked, voluntarily, for the Union of Women. Jen-Eva was a lady of independent means and employed her friend, Margaret, as a secretary cum companion.

"I first met Giles when he came to one of our meetings," began Jen-Eva. "He planned to write a piece for his magazine *Dyke's Progress*. Have you read it at all?"

"No, that one has passed me by I'm afraid," replied Isabel.

"It's a satirical magazine," explained Miss Dunstan. "With a cult following. Giles wrote under the pseudonym *Dyke* and liked to write articles that exposed scandals, fraud and other crime."

"He owns… owned the publication," added Jen-Eva. "His father is a wealthy factory owner. They manufacture sweets, well toffees. You may have heard of Chichester cream fudge. They supply all the best stores. The King is known to like them. His father wanted Giles to follow him into the business, but Giles felt it would be too stifling, preferring to make his own way in his chosen profession. He felt sweet making was demeaning."

But, not the benefit of the profits, thought Isabel.

"Our main priority in the union is to campaign for better wages for female workers," said Miss Dunstan, changing the subject. "That was what Giles wrote about. We are especially concerned about the munitions workers, who do the same jobs as the men, handle the same dangerous materials, but do not receive equal pay. Added to this the TNT has a tendency to discolour their faces yellow. You may have heard them referred to as canaries in some quarters or munitionettes." Miss Hewitt agreed she had. "We also run a laundry for soldiers and advise women on child care, although that is not my area of expertise."

No, thought Isabel. It was obvious Margaret Dunstan was, at heart, a suffragette and a militant one at that. So motherhood might be a low priority for her, but her friend was engaged to be married.

"And Giles Chichester wrote about your work?" Isabel asked.

"He did," agreed Miss Dunstan. "It was an excellent article. Jen-Eva and I were very pleased with it."

"So, did the other exposé articles he wrote make him any enemies?" asked Isabel, anxious to get to the nub of the case and not get bogged down by sweets or suffragette dogma. "Upset someone enough to make them want to kill him?"

Jen-Eva sighed.

"It could have done," she replied.

"He was working on a case about the procuration of young women into prostitution," added Margaret. "He mentioned some man called Derek Sparrow. But that's all we know about it. We have no idea who this man is, or how we can locate him."

"Did you tell the police this?" asked Isabel.

"Of course," replied Jen-Eva, "but Sergeant Perch is of the opinion Giles interrupted a burglary at his rooms. He and I had been dancing at a night club until after 2am. He probably didn't get home much before 3.30. A man was seen running from the building, where he lived, at around 4am. This man collided with a milk cart delivering churns to the dairy. He fell, but managed to get up and ran off, but he left his cap behind. The police have the cap now and are still looking for the man. They think Giles was killed around this time."

"So they have not looked for this Derek Sparrow?"

"Not as far as we know," replied Jen-Eva. "And I don't know how far into the investigation Giles was."

"Has Sergeant Perch found the murder weapon?" asked Isabel. "As I recall The Times reported he was stabbed several times in a frenzied attack."

"No," replied Miss Howard. "As I said, they seem to be making no progress at all." She looked at Isabel. "Do you think you can help us? Money is, of course, no object."

"I can certainly try," replied Isabel, with a smile. "But I will need a few more details, like the address of the magazine and the names of the people, who work there."

"Yes, Giles' partner is Andrew Hilliard. He actually edits the magazine. They publish every fortnight. They have other contributors of course, but the only other members of staff are the illustrator, Jack Forbes, and the secretary, Alice Colman."

"Have you spoken to them about what Giles was working on?" asked Isabel.

"They said they didn't know anything. Giles was always very evasive about his inquiries. Some of his informants liked to remain anonymous. He had to be discreet."

"Of course, I know what it means to be discreet." Isabel made a note of the publication's address in New Fetter Lane. "Did he keep a journal do you know or have a note book?"

"I don't know," sighed Miss Howard. "Actually there's a lot about Giles I don't know. We have only been together for about 6 months."

Isabel nodded.

"How about the milk cart, do you know to which dairy the cart was heading? It might be beneficial to speak to the driver."

"I'm sure Sergeant Perch will advise you of that," suggested Jen-Eva. "We have no idea of any details of that either."

I'm sure he won't, thought Isabel, but didn't say so.

At this point Hattie arrived with the coffee and, as there were biscuits on the tray, Isabel decided the maid should take Pastry down to the kitchen. Otherwise, the pug would beg unreservedly, no doubt focusing her attention on the jittery Miss Dunstan.

CHAPTER TWO

After her visitors had left, Isabel sat down to consider the essentials of their case. If Giles Chichester was involved in some serious crime investigation, his murder, most likely, was connected with that. She knew who might be able to help with finding the elusive Derek Sparrow, but she was concerned about the involvement of Sergeant Perch. Miss Howard had been very dismissive and, certainly, her account of his character was not encouraging. She decided to ring her friend, the lawyer, Hugh Bernard, to find out if he knew anything about the man. Her request was met with an equally discouraging laugh.

"Yes, I know him," said Hugh. "His treble great grandfather was a Bow Street Runner or some such."

"That's the one," sighed Isabel. "So, what am I to expect from him? He's investigating the case I have been engaged to look into."

"He's a buffoon," replied Hugh. "I think he may well have retired, but due to the war, and the shortage of men in the Police Force, he's stayed on. I doubt you'll get any co-operation from him. He's very opposed to women working, let alone investigating crime. These new policewomen patrol officers are a particular object of his ire."

Just my luck thought Isabel. Inspector Mangle of Scotland Yard, with whom she had had most dealings, was usually unreasonable to start with, but eventually came round to her way of thinking. This man sounded as if he wouldn't even speak to her, let alone consider her opinion.

I shall continue regardless, she thought.

She outlined the particulars of the case to Hugh.

"Yes," he said. "That Giles Chichester had a bit of a reputation. I think there might be several people happy to see the back of him."

This case gets just better and better thought Isabel, grimly, and began to regret taking it on.

"I thought I might start with finding out more about this Derek Sparrow and then visit Giles' place of work," she suggested.

"Let me know when you want to go to New Fetter Lane and I'll accompany you," replied Hugh.

"No need," said Isabel. "I shall be quite safe visiting a magazine office."

"I insist," said Hugh. "If they are anything like Giles Chichester, you might need a male escort."

That bad, thought Miss Hewitt with an amused smile and, although sanguine she could acquit herself well enough, agreed to let Hugh attend with her. A second opinion was always helpful, especially from one as astute as Hugh Bernard. And the Hilliard man might open up to a lawyer more than to her.

"I am driving the ambulance this afternoon," she said. "But I am free tomorrow morning."

She hoped Clarke might be back soon. He was a former Metropolitan Police detective and still had one or two friends on the force, if they hadn't already enlisted in the Army. He might be able to discover what the police knew, especially about the driver of the milk cart and if any other witnesses saw the man running away in Stanhope Street. But, if not, she would see him at the hospital that afternoon. Meanwhile, she decided she had time to pay a visit to her friend, Reggie Biddle, in Bayswater.

Reggie was a sharp witted East End boy, with dubious connections and an unspecified occupation. Isabel was the Godmother of his daughter Izzie. He had done good work for her in the past. Hattie drove her to Bayswater in Miss Hewitt's Minerva motor car. Isabel took Pastry, as Reggie and his wife, Tilly, had a soft spot for the pug. They parked close to the ground floor flat, as two trams rattled past, both driven by women. No doubt Sergeant Perch would not approve. Isabel decided she would like to meet this man, even just to establish he was as ridiculous as Hugh claimed. And, of course, she would make sure she wore her WEC uniform when they did!

Reggie still wore the blue uniform of a wounded soldier. Not that he had enlisted, but just wanted to stop people calling him a coward for not doing his bit.

"I really think you should stop wearing that," suggested Isabel, as she sat down in his parlour. "You are a married man with a child, so wouldn't be conscripted anyway. There is no shame in that."

Reggie looked sheepish.

"If you say so, Miss H." He was always anxious to please her. "Now what can I do for you?"

Tilly fussed around Pastry and Hattie played ball on the carpet with little Izzie, who was now walking.

"I have to be brief, Reggie, as I am driving an ambulance this afternoon," explained Isabel. "Do you know a man named Derek Sparrow?"

Reggie considered.

"I've heard of a Derek Sparrow, Miss H. I don't know him."

Miss Hewitt took some money from her purse and handed it over.

"Have this on account. Find out all you can about a man named Derek Sparrow, who may be enticing girls into prostitution. I'd like to know, who he works for, how he operates and where he does it."

Reggie whistled through his teeth.

"That's a lot to ask. I'll have to call in a couple favours. And I don't know if it's the same geezer that I've heard of."

"Sparrow is not all that common a name," replied Isabel. "See what you can dig up Reggie. It's very important. A man has been murdered and

Sparrow may be involved. There will be more money, if you discover what I need to know."

Reggie was too shrewd to ask who had been murdered. What he didn't know, he couldn't be questioned about. And Miss Hewitt was always generous, although he suspected she added her costs to the fees she charged.

"Leave it with me, Miss H. I'll have a word with a few people this afternoon. I'll pop round when I know anything."

Isabel was satisfied. She and Hattie left shortly afterwards.

When they returned to Cartwright Gardens, Isabel found Clarke waiting for her.

"Were there many casualties near Russell Square?" she asked.

He nodded.

"Three families killed. Others injured. It was a direct hit on a house."

Isabel sighed.

"I'm sorry to hear that."

"And I have been in touch with the hospital," he said. "I am to accompany you to the Edmonton. Some seriously injured men need picking up from Waterloo and taken there. Our hospital cannot deal with the injuries."

"Then I will change immediately," replied Isabel. "And we can leave straight after lunch." She looked at Hattie. "You will probably be needed too."

Isabel was pleased to have the chance to travel alone with Clarke. It would give her the opportunity to advise him of the Giles Chichester case and see if he could help with the police.

Isabel left Pastry with her housekeeper, Mrs Rhodes. The woman had grown fond of the pug, except for when she tried to vacuum. But she felt proud that her employer drove a military ambulance and supported her in any way possible.

Clarke sat alongside Isabel as she drove to Waterloo Railway Station with 5 other ambulances, one of which was driven by Hattie. The ambulances were model T Fords, khaki in colour with big red crosses on the side. The seats were not that comfortable and there were no doors, but the WEC uniform was quite thick and the weather was quite mild. Now they were alone, Isabel out lined the details of the case to Clarke. He gave a similar response as Hugh at the mention of Sergeant Perch's name.

"Yes, I know him," he said. "He was my sergeant when I had the trouble." Clarke had been wrongly accused of improper conduct with a senior officer's wife. Although exonerated, he had resigned from the force and, shortly afterwards, had met Isabel. He had worked with her ever since.

"Did he support you?" asked Isabel. "As your sergeant, I would expect he had a duty of loyalty to his men."

"Not a bit," replied Clarke. "He's very strait-laced. If anything, he thought I was guilty of misconduct."

"It wasn't *his* wife, who became obsessed with you was it?" asked Isabel.

Clarke laughed out loud.

"Thankfully, no."

"Hugh described him as a buffoon. Is he that bad?"

Clarke considered.

"I would say dogmatic. Once he has his mind set on something, nothing will shift him. And I doubt he will co-operate with us. But, I still have one friend in the force, Tom Barry. I know he hasn't enlisted, as he is now very short sighted and the army turned him down. I'll go and see him this evening, may be have a pint and a chat in his local. He's helped me before. He'll tell me what the police know."

Now Isabel couldn't wait to lock horns with this dreadful Sergeant. Her rivalry with Inspector Mangle was laced with some good humour. But, she sensed her relationship with Perch might get quite acrimonious. And she objected to him for his behaviour towards Clarke.

Never mind, she thought with a smile. I daresay I will cope better with it than he will!

They picked up the soldiers, some of whom were critically burned and had travelled on a hospital ship and then by train to London. Clarke sat in the back with two casualties and another orderly. Conditions inside were not ideal, being quite cramped. Isabel drove in convoy at a steady 4mph. It was crucial not to jolt the injured, particularly with burns. As she headed for the Edmonton Military Hospital in Silver Street, the occasional moans from her patients made her more aware of soldiers she glimpsed on the streets. There were men on crutches with only one leg, men with no legs in wheelchairs and men who were blind. Some were forced into begging to help support their families. They had survived the trenches, but had paid a dreadful price for their bravery. Examples of this vile conflict seemed everywhere at times, hanging like a toxic spectre on the air, with its grisly fingers wrapped round the throat of the country, trying to strangle its spirit. But, the people showed no signs of giving way and Isabel felt proud to be one of them.

CHAPTER THREE

Clarke returned from his meeting with Tom Barry around ten o'clock. Isabel dozed in her wing chair, as the drama of the previous night was slowly taking effect, with an equally sleepy, Pastry, snoring on her lap.

"Was your old friend any help?" she asked, waking up as he walked in. Pastry immediately jumped off her lap and greeted Clarke with such enthusiasm, as if she hadn't seen him in months. He swept her up in his arms and made a great fuss of her, before sitting down opposite.

"Yes, he is actually working with Sergeant Perch on this and other cases. The Yard are very busy."

They always are thought Isabel.

"Perch is of the opinion the man, who ran into the milk cart, was a burglar. There has been a string of them in that area."

"Is there a description?"

"Yes, according to the driver, the man was well dressed in a fashionable overcoat, and was of slim build. Quite a gentleman, he said."

"Does this tally with the description from the other burglaries?"

Clarke pulled a face.

"There are no other descriptions. No one has seen anything. The burglar, whoever he is, is very crafty, always striking when residents are out."

"So he must watch the houses?"

"It would appear so."

"What does he steal?"

"Usually silver and jewellery and other small, valuable items such as photo frames."

"Was anything stolen from Chichester's flat?"

Clarke shook his head.

"As far as Miss Howard could see nothing was taken."

Isabel considered the situation.

"What about landladies or caretakers? Did Chichester have a landlady?"

"No. The flats in his building are maintained by a caretaker. He discovered the body when he found the flat door open. He saw or heard nothing in the night."

Isabel sighed.

"So the description doesn't mean anything on its own?"

"No, but Perch is convinced the murder is tied up with these other crimes and is not interested in looking elsewhere. I think he wants all the outstanding cases solved."

"How about Derek Sparrow?"

"The police haven't been able to find out anything about him. May be Sparrow is an alias."

"Reggie has heard of a Derek Sparrow, so someone does exist under that name. I plan to pursue that line of inquiry. I'm hoping Reggie will uncover something. He might even know who our crafty burglar is."

"There is one interesting thing, though," said Clarke. "The police have found traces of white cat hair inside a cap the man left behind."

"*Inside?*" queried Isabel. "What are you saying, the cap doubled as a cat basket?"

"Well there was quite a bit of it," replied Clarke with a grin.

"So we have a smart, gentleman burglar, who lets a white cat sleep in his cap." Isabel chuckled. "How bizarre, especially if he regularly wears it and appears to be well dressed. There's a white cat often in the gardens across the road. I hope this burglar doesn't live round here. But, I daresay, there are lots of white cats in London. Did Chichester own one?"

"No," replied Clarke. "The Police have searched his rooms. They found nothing helpful."

"And nothing was stolen. Yet Perch persists with a burglary?"

"He insists the burglar was disturbed before anything could be taken. All the police found was a lot of blood everywhere."

Isabel nodded.

"Quite. So our mystery gentleman may have gone to the rooms with the sole intention of murdering Chichester. Was there any sign of a break in?"

"No, the door hadn't been tampered with, nor had any windows. Then there has been little sign of breaking and entering in the other crimes. They think the burglar picks the locks or has a set of false keys."

"Very clever, if that is the case. But Chichester may have let the man into the flat, which means he may have known him. Did they find anything like a note book or a journal amongst his effects?"

"No."

"He must have made notes in something." Isabel tapped her fingers on the arm of the chair. "They say he was discreet, but he'd need some kind of aide memoir, however cryptic. I'll see if they have it at his office. Did the cart driver say the man was carrying anything? If the murder was connected with something Chichester was working on, the intruder may have taken it."

"It was dark. It all happened so quickly, he didn't see much."

"And The Times reported the attack was quite savage?"

"He was stabbed 27 times," replied Clarke. "The deepest wound was in the back. They think it may have been the first."

"27?" exclaimed Isabel, "and one from behind. That doesn't sound to me like the act of some random burglar, stabbing someone just in order to escape. I mean if Chichester had his back to the assailant, why not just run off before being seen? No this attack was deliberate and indicates passion, so either the intruder was deranged, or they knew Chichester and had some agenda with him. Have they found the murder weapon?"

"No. They believe it was a very sharp knife, possibly one used to cut through meat."

Isabel nodded.

"Such as one most cooks would use in the kitchen. And now it is probably at the bottom of the Thames." She sighed. "Hugh thought there might be several people pleased to see the back of him."

"Tom said Chichester was a gambler. He liked to play poker and roulette. He owed money."

"His creditors wouldn't want him dead, though," said Isabel. "They'd want their money.

No, I reckon he was about to lift the lid on something serious. I'll ask Hugh tomorrow to be more specific, when we go to the *Dyke's Progress* office. Do you have the name of the cart driver?"

"Fred Ames," replied Clarke. "He lives in Camden."

"Excellent," said Isabel. "I think I need to speak to him as well. Yes, we can proceed with what we've discovered, without bothering our blinkered Sergeant Perch. He won't even know we are on the case."

But the blinkered police sergeant would soon find out and object.

The following morning Hattie drove Miss Hewitt and Pastry to Hugh Bernard's office in the city. He was so enamoured of the pug that Isabel had to take her, even though Pastry was suffering from rather disgusting wind. She'd stolen some spicy food from the kitchen and now they were all suffering the after effects! Hugh was ready for them when they arrived. He was a stout man, with a full beard and always wore a top hat to offset his business like suit and frock coat.

"I've taken the precaution of ringing the magazine office and advising them we are calling," he said, climbing into the Minerva.

"Did you tell them our reason for calling?" asked Isabel.

"I was vague," replied Hugh. "A colleague told me that the magazine isn't selling very well and that Andrew Hilliard has had a falling out with Jen-Eva Howard. He may not be that co-operative."

Marvellous, thought Isabel ironically. In that case, I had better leave Pastry in the car. The interview may be stormy enough, without her wind in the equation.

The office of *Dyke's Progress* was a small building resembling a shop, with a large front window, the bottom half of which had a dark green blind with the magazine's name printed across it in large gold letters. It made sure people in the street could not see the staff at work. It reminded Isabel of the cobbler's shop, where she took her shoes to be mended and where local children vainly stood on tip toe trying to see the cobbler at work. They walked inside. The door opened straight into the office area. There were four desks. Andrew Hilliard sat at one, checking some papers and making alterations to the text, whilst the artist Jack Forbes sat at another facing him and drawing an ink caricature from a photograph in a newspaper. The secretary, Alice Colman, sat in the corner typing. The fourth desk, presumably that belonging to Giles Chichester, was not occupied.

Hilliard looked up as they entered. He was a harassed looking young man, with a shock of brown hair in need of a trim. He was in his shirt sleeves and a small pair of round, rimless spectacles perched on his nose. He had a pencil behind his ear. There was an atmosphere of intense activity in the room.

"Can I help you?" he asked. "Mr Bernard, I presume."

He stood up and extended his arm. Hugh shook it.

This looks promising thought Isabel.

"Indeed, sir," replied Hugh, "and may I introduce my colleague, Miss Isabel Hewitt."

The polite atmosphere immediately shifted. Hilliard stiffened.

"Miss Hewitt, yes. If you have been sent here by Miss Jen-Eva Howard, then I have nothing to say to you. I know who you are and that she has consulted you. She boasted as such on the telephone yesterday."

Isabel smiled politely, ignoring the rebuke.

"I have to say, Mr Hilliard, Miss Howard has not *sent* me here or anywhere else, come to that. Yes, I have been engaged by her to find the killer of your partner, Giles Chichester, but have decided to call on you of my own volition. I thought you may like to assist in getting justice for your friend."

He shrugged.

"The police are dealing with it."

"Indeed. The police think he disturbed a burglar. That is one explanation, but I think there might be another."

"Perhaps we could sit down, Hilliard," suggested Hugh, with a hard edge to his voice. "Where are your manners, sir?"

Jack Forbes immediately stood up and offered Isabel his seat, which she accepted with a polite smile. Forbes was a slightly built, almost feminine looking man, with light brown, long hair tied back in a pigtail and fixed with a leather ring. His features were delicate and his hands, small. They were littered with ink stains from his sketching. Hilliard was momentarily shame faced, but made no apology and took his seat behind his desk.

"Very well, Miss Hewitt, what is your other explanation? But I must warn you that I have no intention of allowing Miss Howard, or her dreary friend Miss Dunstan, anywhere near this magazine office again. She had the impertinence to think she could take over Giles's share of the business. Help with the editorial. They even tried to suggest Alice, here, was not being paid enough."

"Then, indeed," agreed Isabel, "that was impertinent and you are justified in being angry and I have no intention of suggesting any such thing. I am more interested in finding out what Giles was working on before he was killed."

"I see. Jen-Eva wants to know about that does she, so she can write the article herself. This publication has standards, Miss Hewitt. It is not a vehicle for amateurs or for suffragette propaganda."

"Mr Hilliard," said Isabel succinctly, "if you could put your animosity about Miss Howard to one side for a moment, have you considered that

Giles Chichester was murdered to keep him quiet? That the case he was working on was so dangerous, they killed him. And having done that, the killers might come after you also, as you were partners and might be privy to the same information?" It was clear Andrew Hilliard had not considered any such thing, so Isabel decided to call his bluff. "Then I suggest that you furnish me with whatever information you can, so I may track them down before they find you."

There was a stunned silence in the office. Alice Colman had stopped typing. She darted an alarmed glance at Jack Forbes. The artist, who was perched on his desk, having given his chair to Miss Hewitt, stood up and marched across to the empty desk. He unlocked a drawer from a key on a bunch he pulled from his pocket. He removed a black leather bound loose leaf note book. He handed it to Isabel.

"Here, Miss Hewitt, Giles made all his notes in this. They probably won't make much sense, as he liked to write in some kind of code. I have never been able to decipher it. But please see if this helps."

"Thank you," said Isabel .She looked askance at Hilliard. "You didn't think to hand this over to the police?"

He shrugged again.

"They didn't ask for it."

Isabel slipped the notebook into her bag.

"Extraordinary," she muttered.

"Are we finished?" he said brusquely. "I have a magazine to edit."

Hugh bridled at the rudeness, but Isabel was equal to it.

"Indeed we are," she replied, rising to her feet. She glanced at Jack. "Thank you for your co-operation." She looked at Hilliard. "And I am sorry you appear so indifferent to obtaining justice for your late partner. But, if I track down the killer before he gets to you, rest assured, you will be the first to know. Good day to you."

And she swept out of the office before Hilliard had the chance to reply, secretly wishing she had taken Pastry inside with her, so the pug could have broken wind and left the insufferable man with the offensive smell!

"Arrogant young pup!" growled Hugh as they walked up the pavement to where the Minerva was parked. "Such rudeness was insupportable."

"Yes, his attitude was quite extraordinary," replied Isabel. "Whatever has Jen-Eva done to incur such contempt?"

Before they could climb into the car, a voice called 'Miss Hewitt' from behind them. Isabel and Hugh turned and saw the artist, Jack Forbes, emerging from an alley way running down beside the magazine premises.

"Mr Forbes?" said Isabel. "Can I help you?"

"I feel I ought to explain and apologise for Andy," he said. "He is not usually so curmudgeonly. He *is* upset by Giles' death, but was also angry with his friend."

"Go on," said Isabel.

"Giles was engaged to Andy's sister Amelia. They were due to marry this summer. Then he met Jen-Eva Howard and just broke off the engagement. Andy accused him of jilting her, because Jen-Eva is a wealthy heiress and, to be fair, Giles was always short of money."

"What did Giles say?"

"He denied it, of course."

"But you believe it to be true?"

Jack was suddenly flustered and his cheeks coloured.

"It is not my place to judge Giles, but Amelia is a delightful, young woman. I cannot understand why he should prefer Miss Howard."

I daresay Amelia Hilliard is not as wealthy as Miss Howard, thought Isabel. He probably loved neither. She was beginning to dislike this man.

"Does Miss Hilliard live in London?" she asked.

"No, in Eastbourne, but please don't divulge I have told you about the break up. Amelia is still heart broken. And she still loved Giles, so his death has hit her very badly."

"Quite," said Isabel. The man was obviously in love with the girl himself. "Now what was Giles's position in the business?"

"He owned it," replied Jack. "To start with Andy was just the editor. He and Giles were friends from their Oxford days. Giles liked to write most of the copy. He was good, witty and sometimes controversial. He hired me as his illustrator. I also take photographs. But the magazine didn't sell that well. And Giles was in some financial difficulty. He had a falling out with his father, who stopped his allowance. So Andy bought into it and became a partner. He introduced new sales techniques and the circulation improved. He was also able to rein Giles in on some of the stories. We'd had one or two close shaves with the libel laws."

Hugh nodded.

"Yes, a colleague advised me of that."

"Was anyone sufficiently offended to want Chichester dead?" asked Isabel.

Jack shook his head.

"Everything was ended quite amicably. Andy is a good businessman, unlike Giles. He was able to smooth things over. Giles didn't really have a head for business. He just wanted to write. He founded the magazine mainly for that reason. But I must get back. I just wanted to apologise for Andy."

"Thank you for your concern," said Isabel. She looked at Hugh as the artist hurried back up the alleyway. "Well, well, a jilted lover and libel suits, Giles Chichester led a colourful life." She held up the note book. "Let's hope this gives up some of his secrets."

"And there is another possible suspect," suggested Hugh.

"Or two," replied Isabel. "Miss Hilliard may have a champion in her brother and Jack Forbes. The severity of the attack could be a crime of passion. But we shall see."

They climbed into the Minerva.

"Afraid the pug's been dropping a few," apologised Hattie, "and her stomach is gurgling."

"Let's walk her in Green Park before we go home," suggested Isabel.

CHAPTER FOUR

Back at Cartwright Gardens, Isabel was able to examine Giles Chichester's note book. Jack Forbes was right, the handwriting was hard to decipher. It was written in pencil and more like illegible scribble. The man hadn't adopted a code, just a slovenly writing style. But she was able to pick out a name, Mavis Higgins, with an address in Islington. There was also the word canary by the name. But, more tellingly, the words Derek Sparrow were circled twice. She showed it to Hugh, who had accepted Isabel's offer of lunch.

"In the absence of any other firm information, I think we should pay a call on this woman," suggested Isabel. Hugh agreed and, as he felt Islington was not a very salubrious place for Isabel to visit alone, he insisted he accompany her. Hattie was driving an ambulance that afternoon, but Isabel was not required.

"You must have other, more pressing work," said Isabel.

"No. This is a murder investigation and your safety is paramount, especially as Giles Chichester may have been murdered for dabbling in this case."

Isabel accepted his offer and was grateful for it; although she made sure she carried her father's revolver, secreted in her bag.

She drove to the address in Islington. They took Pastry, whose digestive problems had eased and parked a little way up the street from the narrow, terraced house. As usual the street teemed with people, some walking purposefully to their destination, others loafing menacingly.

"You stay with Pastry in the car, Hugh," said Isabel. "I don't want the Minerva getting damaged. I shall be quite safe and won't go in the house if I suspect it might be dangerous."

Isabel knocked the door. She heard a movement inside and saw the curtains twitch.

"Who are you?" said a woman's voice, moments later.

"Mavis Higgins?" queried Isabel.

"As I said, who are you?" came the sharp reply.

"My name is Isabel Hewitt and I am here about Giles Chichester."

"I ain't saying nothing," replied the woman.

"I will pay you for any information," continued Isabel, "if you open the door." She opened her purse and removed two half crowns.

There was a heavy pause, then the bolts were slid aside and the woman opened the door just a crack. Isabel saw a pretty, young woman with a yellow complexion, a fresh scar on the side of her cheek in a shabby dress and with bandaged hands. She schooled her expression to hide her shock.

"Miss Higgins?"

"Yes. What do you want?"

"I see you are a munitions worker."

"Was," replied the woman. "Can't work with these hands."

Isabel's brow creased.

"What happened?" She looked at the scar. "Who did this to you?"

"I got this for talking to Giles Chichester," said Mavis. "Now he's copped it, too. I ain't saying nothing."

"Did Derek Sparrow do this?" Mavis Higgins' expression was suddenly guarded, which told Isabel she knew the name. The woman was poised to say something, when a big, loutish man suddenly loomed beside Miss Hewitt. He stank of beer, sweat and unwashed underclothes.

"What's going on?" he growled, pushing himself between Isabel and the door. "You all right, Mave?"

"Yes, Alfie," replied the woman. "This lady was only giving me some money."

"Oh yeah?" said the man. "You can give it me."

"I certainly shall not!" said Isabel briskly, seeing Hugh approaching from behind him. "Now, stand aside!"

The man was not used to a woman speaking back to him and such a stylish young woman at that. He moved sufficiently for Isabel to hand the woman the half crowns. She snatched them with her bandaged hands and slipped the money into her dress pocket, muttering *five bob*.

"Thank you, Miss Higgins," Isabel said, as Hugh joined her at the door. Hugh fixed the man with a steely glance as if daring him to resort to violence, which Isabel thought rather reckless. But it had the desired effect.

"Look what they did to her!" growled the man. "Smashed her hands they did, for talking to that Giles geezer. He gave her money, too."

"Who did? Who did this?" demanded Isabel.

"Just get out if it!" roared the man. He went to raise his hand. Hugh pulled Isabel away.

"We're leaving," he said and, without another word, took her by the arm and hurried back to the Minerva. Thankfully the oaf did not follow them. Hugh cranked the starting handle and Isabel drove off, although she found she shook so much initially she could hardly steer or fuss Pastry, who as usual, was delighted to see her.

"Thank you, Hugh," she said, as her composure began to return the further she drove from the address.

"Did you find out anything?" asked Hugh, still somewhat shaken, himself. Isabel nodded.

"I suspect that woman was Chichester's informant. She recognised the name Derek Sparrow. She was beaten up for talking to him. Someone has cut her face and broken her hands." She changed gear as they approached a junction. "Whoever these people are, they are very dangerous. I suspect even that oaf, Alfie, was scared. It's looking more likely *they* killed Giles Chichester. Now all we have to do is find out who they are."

"Are you sure it is safe to do that?" said Hugh.

"No," said Isabel. "But that has never stopped me before."

Isabel drove Hugh back with her to Cartwright Gardens. Both agreed a restorative brandy would be in order. But when she arrived, Isabel found her housekeeper, Mrs Rhodes, in an agitated state.

"There is a rather unpleasant man waiting to see you," she said. "He's been here half an hour. I put him in the sitting room. He wouldn't give his name."

Isabel's heart missed a beat. Was it Derek Sparrow? Had he discovered they were enquiring about him already? With Hugh at her elbow and Pastry in her arms, she walked boldly into the sitting room. A grey haired, lugubrious looking man, with a large drooping moustache and hairy side whiskers turned to greet her. He wore an iron grey frock coat and had a starched, pristine wing collar. He cut quite a Victorian figure with his highly polished shoes and iron grey spats. He scowled.

"At last." He pulled a gold, hunter pocket watch from his iron grey waistcoat. "I have been here a full 32 minutes."

"My apologies," replied Isabel, politely. "Had I know you were calling Mr er..

"The name's Perch," he replied briskly. "*Detective Sergeant* Perch from Scotland Yard."

Isabel darted a glance at the framed photograph of Clarke hanging on the wall, beside a matching one of her. Had he noticed it and recognised his former detective constable, whom he had thought capable of inappropriate behaviour?

"Then, good morning," she replied, school her expression to appear cordial. "I believe you know my associate Hugh Bernard." He grunted and Hugh merely nodded. "And do sit down Sergeant." She let Pastry down onto the floor and the pug ran immediately to sniff the visitor.

"No thank you, Madam, I prefer to stand, for what I have to say will not take long. And call your dog off. To my mind, animals have no place in a house and definitely not in a sitting room."

That's me told, thought Isabel.

She decided to sit down and called Pastry across to her. She then deliberately put the dog on her lap and smiled politely again. Hugh stood behind her.

"Now Sergeant, what can I do for you?"

"It has been drawn to my attention," began Perch with a sententious pomposity, "that you claim to be investigating the death of Giles Chichester?"

"I have been asked to do so by Miss Howard, Mr Chichester's fiancée," replied Isabel, wondering who had told him. It had to be someone from the magazine, or was it Clarke's old friend?

"Then I insist you stop," he said. "Police work is for properly trained male officers. It is not for bungling amateurs, nor women."

"Now, mind your language, Perch," said Hugh.

Isabel refused to be drawn.

"I may be a woman," she replied, calmly, "but I am no bungling amateur. Ask your superior, Inspector Mangle."

Perch glowered.

"The Inspector is not on this case, I am. How he chooses to work is his business. I will not bandy words with you, Madam. I am telling you to stop meddling in my investigation. I come from a long line of police officers and, nowhere is there indication that women have a part to play."

Isabel begged to differ, but couldn't be bothered to argue.

"Have you found Derek Sparrow?" she asked almost with an air of insolence.

He bridled at the question.

"That, Madam, is none of your business."

Isabel removed the notebook from her bag.

"Really? Perhaps you would like to read this, Sergeant. It is Giles Chichester's aide memoir. In it he mentions a Mavis Higgins, who lives in Islington. We have just spoken to her and she has been badly beaten for talking to him. He was working on something dangerous and this Derek Sparrow is involved." She held up the note book. "Perhaps you would like to have it as evidence?"

He snorted. His anger was mounting.

"Evidence! Don't tell me what I should treat as evidence! Giles Chichester was a chancer, who wrote mostly made up stories for that magazine of his. I doubt any of them were true and I also doubt anything in that book has a bearing on this case. Chichester disturbed a burglar!"

"So, how do you explain this woman and her injuries?"

"No doubt she has a man in her life and, probably, a drunken, violent one at that. I have been doing this job a long time Madam, I daresay before you were born. I know what these people are like. Now I'm warning you, leave the detective work to me."

"And if I don't?" said Isabel.

He almost exploded with rage.

"Then, Madam, I shall arrest you!"

"You can't do that!" objected Hugh. "Miss Hewitt is not breaking the law!"

"Yes, on what charge?" asked Isabel.

Perch glared his face puce with anger, as he strode across the room towards the sitting room door.

"An appropriate one, Madam, good day to you."

"One moment," said Isabel, moderating her tone. "I agree. I will not interfere with your detective work. It is your case, Sergeant and I respect that."

Her words took him completely by surprise. He looked at her dumbfounded, then, with just an unintelligible snort, flung open the door. Mrs Rhodes stood outside, fearful for her mistress. He swept past her without a glance, and out into the street, slamming the front door behind him. Pastry, who had fallen asleep on Isabel's lap, woke up and barked.

"Well, well!" said Isabel, letting the pug jump onto the floor. "That was interesting."

"You see what I mean about a buffoon," said Hugh.

Isabel considered.

"May be, but I think he feels his authority is being threatened. As you say, if it wasn't for the war, he may well have retired. Times have changed and, I daresay, he hasn't."

"Are you going to give up on the case?" asked Hugh.

"Not at all," replied Isabel. "You heard him say he isn't interested in Derek Sparrow, so there is nothing to stop me from following that up." She paused. "Although, he may have a point about Mavis Higgins having a violent boyfriend. That Alfie character looked rather like a bruiser to me."

At this point Mrs Rhodes, white faced, walked nervously into the room.

"Did I do right letting him in, Ma'am?" she asked. "I wasn't sure."

"Yes, yes, he was only Sergeant Perch from Scotland Yard," replied Isabel with a smile. "Of course you did the right thing."

The housekeeper gave a sigh of relief and almost swayed on her feet.

"I'll get us all a brandy," said Hugh.

"Yes," agreed Isabel, standing up. "Come and sit down Mrs Rhodes. You look like you need one more than we do!"

But, they had hardly taken a sip, when there was a knock on the front door. Was this Perch, back to have another row with them?

CHAPER FIVE

"I'll go," said Hugh, equally concerned it might be Perch again. But, moments later, he brought Reggie Biddle into the sitting room.

"That copper has gone hasn't he, Miss H?" he asked anxiously. "I saw him arrive. I went for a walk about, as I didn't want him to see me."

"Yes, he has just left," replied Isabel. Reggie looked hopefully at the brandy glasses. "Pour Reggie one, Hugh," she said. "I assume he has some information for us."

"Shall I go Ma'am?" asked Mrs Rhodes, whose colour was only just returning, as the restorative properties of the brandy took effect.

"No, stay," said Isabel, "until you feel quite recovered." She looked at Reggie, as he sat down in the wing chair opposite, "now, any news?"

"First, I have to say I'm not a copper's nark," he said.

"Of course not," replied Isabel. "Anything you say will be for our ears only."

Reggie was satisfied.

"I've found out something about this geezer, Derek Sparrow. That ain't his real name, but I don't know what is."

"Go on," said Isabel, as Hugh handed Reggie a generous brandy. He did seem rather agitated, which was not like him.

"There's some swindle going on with a butchers in Highbury. Morgan's Meats it is, round the corner off Gillespie Road. The owner, Bert Morgan, runs it by himself, as his two sons are away in the army. He always seems to have the best cuts of meat and sells them off cheap. So, there's always a long queue outside his shop, often an hour before he opens. He don't do that till ten and he closes at 1 o'clock. He's raking in the cash, too, but no one knows where he gets his meat from."

"How is this connected with Derek Sparrow?" asked Isabel.

"I'm coming to that," replied Reggie, finishing the brandy and looking for a refill. Isabel nodded and Hugh obliged. "That's where Sparrow picks up the girls. He goes down the queue and chooses the pretty, young ones, the ones whose husbands or fiancés are either killed, or away fighting."

"How does he pick them up? How does he know who to approach?"

"Don't know, Miss H. But he somehow offers them something and then traps them into some kind of immorality."

"Is it something to do with meat?" asked Isabel intrigued.

"That I don't know either," said Reggie, "May be he just finds the queue handy. But he seems to like canaries, you know them girls from the munitions. If there's one of them in the queue, he always goes after them. And the word is he likes a girl with a bit of back chat."

Isabel's brow creased with a frown.

"Why canaries?"

"More exotic, Miss H."

"Disgusting," muttered Hugh, "exploiting women, who do such good work."

Isabel agreed in principal.

"But, this all sounds very bizarre, Reggie. It isn't something Giles Chichester has put about is it, just to get a story for his magazine?"

But, a butcher would use a sharp meat knife.

"No, Miss H, this is straight up. The geezer who told me said there's some nasty people behind it. That's all I know."

"I have heard of Morgan's Meats," said Mrs Rhodes, now feeling quite recovered. "The customers at my butchers often say it might be worth trying, if they wanted a good bit of steak for a special occasion. And it's just down the road from the underground." She looked at Isabel. "Perhaps I could go along there and see what I can find out. If the meat is as good as they say, we can all eat well on it."

"It might be dangerous," said Hugh.

"This man isn't going to be interested in me," said Mrs Rhodes, chuckling. "I am way too old."

"But he might be interested in *me*," said Isabel.

"No," objected Hugh.

"I can act just as the bait," continued Isabel. "I can even colour my face yellow. I'm sure there is some theatrical make up that would do the trick. That way I can find out what Sparrow offers to lure the girls in. I don't have to take up the offer. And it may be a way of finding who's behind it."

"It might be risky, Miss H," warned Reggie. "You shouldn't go on your own."

"I shall go with you, Ma'am," said Mrs Rhodes. "I'd like to buy some meat!"

"No, I meant having a man about. I'll come along. I've a friend in Highbury. I support the Arsenal. see. I can always make out I'm seeing him."

"You must tell Clarke, too," insisted Hugh.

"Then we'll all go," said Isabel with a smile. "Clarke has a day off tomorrow. But I will need to visit the theatrical costumiers this afternoon to get the make-up."

Arrangements were made with Reggie to be at the butcher's shop the next day at 9 o'clock. Isabel offered him lunch, but he declined. He was quite jittery, not like him at all. This Derek Sparrow and his operation, although it sounded far-fetched, certainly scared anyone associated with it.

After lunch Isabel drove Hugh back to his office. Hattie and Clarke were still not back from their shifts. Then she went to a theatrical costumier near Goodge Street, where her friend, the male impersonator Dilly Gosling, always bought her stage make up. She was able to purchase some yellow base grease paint and removal cream. Also she hired a black wig.

"Doing a performance of the Mikado?" asked the man behind the counter. "That yellow is really good. It's the latest. We've only just had it in."

"Something like that," replied Isabel and left before he could ask her any further questions.

That evening Clarke was not happy.

"It is too dangerous," he told Isabel.

"I shall be fine," she replied. "I won't get myself into any compromising position. And, of course, I will be disguised."

"Then, I shall come with you," he insisted.

"Very well, but you must stay in the background. I shall leave Pastry here with Hattie. I can't take *her* into a butcher's shop with the smell of all that meat. Mrs Rhodes and I will travel by underground. You can bring the Minerva and park near by, just in case." She consulted her underground map. "The Electric Piccadilly line takes us straight to Gillespie Road."

Clarke had no choice, but agree.

Isabel was up very early the next morning. After washing she sat at her dressing table mirror and began applying the base yellow make up. She smoothed it as evenly as she could. Hattie was on hand to help. After Isabel was satisfied she resembled a canary colour, she powdered her face in the hope of concealing the grease paint. And she added bright lipstick and rouge to deflect attention from it also. She had some shabby clothes she had used before. She put these on and then the wig. She looked at herself in the mirror. A perfect stranger stared back at her.

Perfect, she thought.

Clarke was quite shocked when he saw her.

"Can you see the greasepaint?" she asked.

"The powder is camouflaging it well enough, and the rouge," he said. "But you can just see the yellow showing through."

"That's just the effect I want," she said.

Isabel wore a knitted scarf wrapped round her neck, though she wore a high necked blouse. Suddenly she felt less sanguine about pulling off the deceit. What if Sparrow smelled the grease paint? She smothered herself in cheap, pungent perfume, hoping to mask it. She asked Hattie what she thought.

"You look like someone I don't know," replied the maid.

Mrs Rhodes arrived shortly afterwards. She, too, was quite shocked to see her mistress looking like some common tart. They explained the plan to her. After both had bought some meat and, hopefully, Isabel had spoken to Sparrow, they would head back to the underground station, where Clarke would follow at a distance and pick them both up in the Minerva.

The underground was busy. They caught a train from Kings Cross on the Piccadilly Line and alighted at Gillespie Road, the station nearest the butchers. Isabel walked in front with Mrs Rhodes following, as if they were not together. They walked past the rows of terraces houses in the opposite direction to the Arsenal Football stadium. They turned into Blackstock Road and arrived at the shop, on the opposite pavement, just after 9 o'clock. The queue was already forming, consisting mainly of older matronly women with baskets. There were men around, but no-one appeared to be taking an interest in the queue. Isabel saw Reggie loafing on a corner with a small suitcase, as if he was a street seller. There were one or two other young women waiting. Clarke stood on the corner of Gillespie Road reading a newspaper. The Minerva was parked out of sight.

"You been here before?" asked one woman, standing just in front of Isabel. Isabel felt she'd been further up the line, but had dropped back to talk to her. She was a grubby looking woman with a large basket on her arm.

"Nah," she replied, feigning a common accent. "Just fancied a bit of good meat tonight. It's me Ma's birthday. Heard it was the best around, here."

"He'll only let you have one piece," replied the woman. "Mean old skinflint he is. He says he has to be fair on everyone. But the best cuts go first. I'm here from Stepney."

"Camden me," said Isabel, which was where Mrs Rhodes lived.

"Not working then?" said the woman. "You're in munitions ain't you?"

"Day off," replied Isabel. "Ma's birthday."

The woman paused and looked at Isabel. Had she noticed the grease paint?

"Why does it turn your skin yellow?" The woman was prying now.

"TNT," replied Isabel, "and I ain't supposed to talk about it. Top secret see. War effort."

"Just you and your Ma at home is it?" continued the woman.

"Yeah. Me fiancé is in France."

"No little 'uns then?"

"Do us a favour, Missus," replied Isabel. "I ain't wed yet."

The woman nodded. Then, moments later, a raddled faced, scruffy middle aged man, smoking a thin rolled up cigarette, strolled past the queue. He wore a shabby suit and filthy cap. When he approached the spot where Isabel stood, he suddenly coughed and spat on the pavement.

"Oi!" said Isabel, remembering what Reggie had said about back chat. "Mind your manners you dirty beggar. I don't want your germs!"

The offensive man bridled.

"You watch your mouth, woman." He appraised her with his gimlet eyes. "You're one of them canaries ain't you? Just because you do a man's job, don't mean you can speak to me like that. Women should be at home looking after their menfolk, not working in factories."

"I do a good job!" retorted Isabel. "It's me doing my bit for the war, ain't it?"

"Pah!" The man was dismissive. He smelled of cigarettes and sweat and his breath was foul.

"You up to date with your German then?" asked Isabel insolently. "If we don't make the ammunition, we'll lose the war, then you'll need it when the Hun invade."

"Why you…" The man raised his hand to slap her, but the woman in front intervened.

"That's enough Ike Giggle. Leave her be. She's doing no harm. Her man's fighting In France."

Isabel saw Reggie, too, had made a move to approach the queue. She had already stepped back, anticipating the blow. The man thought better of it and shambled off down the street.

"Behave, Miss," objected Mrs Rhodes behind her, beginning to fear her mistress was going too far. "You know what some men are like."

"Yeah, sorry, Missus," said Isabel. She glanced over her shoulder to watch Ike Giggle walk down the queue looking at everyone. A more inappropriately named man she had yet to meet. Reggie had strolled down the street behind him and had stopped opposite Gillespie Road.

Isabel had a feeling Giggle might be something to do with it, but, she was sure he wasn't Derek Sparrow.

Suddenly there was a movement up ahead.

"Shop's open," said the woman standing in front. "Better make sure no one pushes in."

The queue suddenly became more orderly with everyone focused on getting into the shop. Isabel felt her pulse quicken. Would she be able to spring the trap on Derek Sparrow, or would he smell a rat?

CHAPTER SIX

The queue moved slowly. There was a bit of pushing at the back, but Isabel and Mrs Rhodes stood their ground. At last they reached the shop door. A notice said: **ONE PURCHASE PER CUSTOMER**. Behind it various carcases hung in the window, for customers to select their cuts of meat.

"Get a bit of rump," whispered Mrs Rhodes. "I'll see if I can get fillet."

Bob Morgan was a bald-headed man of about 50 in a blood stained apron, who looked very pleased with himself. His shop was quite large inside and the floor was covered in sawdust. There was a lot of meat on display. A wizened little Chinese man worked in the background chopping more cuts of meat on a blood stained block. Bob smiled at the woman in front of Isabel.

"Morning, Mrs Giggle. The usual is it?"

Giggle thought Isabel. You're that foul oaf's wife.

The woman bought her meat, turned, and walked out of the shop. Then it was Isabel's turn.

"Yes, love?" said Bob. "What can I get you?"

"Nice bit of rump please, mate," replied Isabel. She pointed to a very lean cut on display. "I'll have that one."

"Good choice, love," said the butcher.

As Bob Morgan wrapped her purchase, Isabel was aware of a figure moving out of the shadows to her right.

This might be it, she thought. As she turned to leave with her meat, the figure stepped forward.

"Got a minute love?" he said. Isabel saw he was a well dressed, stocky man with jet black, slick backed hair and a small, thin moustache. He smelled of cigars and strong hair oil.

"What you want?" she asked, appearing outwardly calm but in reality her heart hammered.

He nodded to the purchase in her hand.

"Pleased with your meat?"

She grinned.

"Course. Looks a nice bit of rump, Mister."

"Shame you can't get more," he said.

"Yeah, Wouldn't have minded some beef sausages an' all. Me Ma likes a bit of beef sausage."

"Well then, how would you like to have as much meat as you like?"

"What do you mean?" asked Isabel.

The man gave an oily smile.

"Actually I supply all the meat here. I like to help out certain customers. You're obviously a munitions worker doing her bit for the war. I'd like to reward you."

"Really, Mister?"

"Yes." He handed her a small business card. "If you call at the rear of the restaurant on this card any evening after 7 and say Derek sent you, you can buy all the meat you like at the same prices as here. Just go up the alley at the side of the building and you'll come to a gate with the restaurant's name on it. Ring the bell and someone will answer it."

Isabel read the name on the card.

"The Silver Platter, Cambridge Square. Ain't that up West?"

"You can get there on the tube quite easily. Where do you live?"

"Camden. Near the tube station actually."

"Not too far out then."

"No. Right oh, Mister. I'll call round tomorrow after I finish me shift. Ma likes her meat, bless her."

"What's your name?" asked the man. "So they'll know in the meat store."

"Oh yeah. Phyllis Crow. And you're Derek you said."

He gave the same oily smile.

"Yes. Derek Sparrow."

Isabel gave a cackle.

"Me Crow, you Sparrow quite a couple of old birds ain't we? Tata, mate."

He laughed mirthlessly.

I'm annoying him, good, thought Isabel and walked jauntily out of the shop. Mrs Rhodes had already left and was walking slowly towards Gillespie Road. Clarke was no longer in view and Reggie loafed on the opposite corner. Isabel set off towards Gillespie Road herself and turned the corner. She noticed Reggie had moved ahead and now crossed over to her side of the pavement. Ike Giggle watched her from a shop doorway, another thin, rolled up cigarette drooping from the corner of his disagreeable mouth.

Isabel began walking up towards the underground station. Mrs Rhodes, up ahead, was almost there. Reggie suddenly accosted her.

"Wanna buy some trinkets, lady?" He opened his case to reveal watches, necklaces and other jewellery all winking in the sunlight. Isabel just gawped amazed. "You're being followed," he whispered. "Don't look now. It's that man from the queue, the one who spat. He went round the back of the shop after he spoke to you, so he's in on it. I'll hold him up, whilst you hurry to the station. Reckon he plans to follow you home, so they'll know where you live."

"Thanks Reggie," said Isabel.

"Mr Clarke has the car parked round the corner. Give that man the slip in the station. He's with the woman, who talked to you in the queue. She's already gone up."

Isabel nodded she understood.

"No, don't want nothing, mate," she said in a loud voice. She set off up Gillespie Road, but pretended to turn to look at Reggie. She saw Ike Giggle had also stopped, but was now about to walk after her.

"Want to buy any trinkets, mate," said Reggie, blocking Giggle's way. "Something nice and shiny for your old lady. Really cheap, but good quality."

Ike Giggle scowled.

"No, get out of my way you oaf."

"Won't take a minute, mate. Just have a look. I've some really good pieces. Won't get anything like this any cheaper."

"I said, no!" growled Giggle.

But, Reggie would not let him past. Eventually, just as Isabel reached the underground station,

Giggle finally shook him off. Isabel concealed herself behind a notice board. She saw the man hurry in. He looked round, but didn't see her. So he headed for the train platforms. When she was satisfied he'd gone, she nipped back outside. Clarke was just down the road in the Minerva with the engine running. She ran down to the car and jumped inside.

"Lay flat," he said. "Just in case that man comes out as we're leaving."

But, as they drove away, Giggle was still scouring the crowded platform. A lot of people headed back into London. Mrs Rhodes waited patiently. She saw the woman from the queue standing nearby, and then she saw Ike Giggle stop and speak to her. The woman shook her head. Giggle then spoke to other passengers, including Mrs Rhodes.

"You seen one of them canaries, you know munitions workers, on the platform?"

"No, love," replied Ms Rhodes. "There's none of them factories round here."

"She was at the butchers," replied Giggle.

"Oh right."

"If you do see her, point her in my direction," said Ike. "She dropped her purse."

"If I see her, I'll tell her," replied Mrs Rhodes.

At this point the train arrived at the platform. Mrs Rhodes climbed into a carriage and saw Giggle and his wife get on the train a carriage further down. She decided to get off at Caledonian Road and catch a later train, just in case the pair tried to follow her, but they didn't. She was able to return to Cartwright Gardens unobserved, already planning how she was going to cook the meat. And she knew Isabel had a nice bit of rump, too. All in all it had been quite an interesting morning and she was very impressed with her mistress's acting skills. When she first took the job with Miss Hewitt, she hadn't expected it to be anything more than housekeeping. But it was proving to be quite a challenge, especially with a clumsy maid like Hattie in the kitchen, dropping the china on the floor.

Back at Cartwright Gardens, Isabel removed the greasepaint and changed her clothes, whilst Clarke put the meat in the cool pantry. Pastry was very interested in the purchase, but only managed to beg a dog biscuit. Then Clarke rang Hugh Bernard to see if he knew anything about the Silver Platter restaurant. Isabel had heard of it, as it was very fashionable and patronised by the wealthy.

"They have to be," she said, "at the prices they charge."

"It's owned by a Georgio Sampras," said Hugh. "But I don't know anymore. I've never dined there."

By the time Mrs Rhodes returned, Isabel and Clarke sat in the sitting room drinking coffee and discussing the case. Neither had seen anyone, who fitted the description of the man seen running from Giles Chichester's rooms. Giggle was too small and the man claiming to be Derek Sparrow was too stocky. But someone like Georgio Sampras would have others to do his dirty work for him. It was looking likely that they were on the right trail.

"Were you followed?" asked Isabel.

"No," replied Mrs Rhodes and explained how she swopped trains. "That dirty man came looking for you. He got on the train with that nosey woman from the queue."

"Good. And now he'll be scouring Camden looking for Phyllis Crow," said Isabel. "Disgusting individual. Well done Mrs Rhodes."

"I'd better go and start preparing lunch," replied the housekeeper. "And put the meat away."

"No. Have a coffee before you do that," said Isabel. "I'll get Hattie to put the meat away and get another cup."

Later, Isabel considered her next move with Clarke.

"They've done nothing wrong, just offered me cheap meat," she said. "It's what happens at the restaurant, when the girls take up the offer, that's the key. I'll just have to chance it and go along there."

"I don't think you should," suggested Clarke. "They'll be suspicious. You gave Giggle the slip. The fact they don't know your address might make them wary. It's obviously part of the swindle. They can exert more pressure, if they know where you live. They can threaten your family."

Isabel nodded.

"That's true. But I've found out this much. I can't just leave it."

"They are dangerous people. Look what they did to Mavis Higgins."

"Yes, Mavis Higgins," said Isabel. "May be she can tell us how it works, if she'll speak to me that is. She's the link with Chichester. We'll go and see her after lunch." She paused. "And Reggie had a whole suitcase full of jewellery and watches. They looked the real thing. I wonder where they came from?"

"You don't think he's Sergeant Perch's burglar do you?" said Clarke with a half-smile.

Isabel looked alarmed.

"I hope not!" But how Reggie earned his living had always been a mystery. "No," she said. "I don't want to think about that!"

CHAPTER SEVEN

Hattie drove them both to Islington after lunch. Isabel decided to take Pastry with her. A woman with a cute little dog might appear less of a threat. She hoped Mavis Higgins would be in and the bruiser, Alfie, would not. With any luck, he would still be in the pub. Mavis was not pleased to see her.

"You again!" she said. "I ain't got anything to say."

"It is important I speak with you," replied Isabel. She held up the card Sparrow gave her. "I know about the butcher, Morgan's Meats, and Derek Sparrow. What will happen if I take up his offer at this restaurant?"

The woman's eyes widened in horror.

"You mustn't, Miss. It's dangerous."

"Why is it dangerous?"

"It's a trick and they are nasty people."

"Then tell me all about it. Let me in. I'll pay you for information."

"You ain't a copper?" asked Mavis.

"No," replied Isabel. "Someone has asked me to find the killer of Giles Chichester. I think it is something to do with this meat business. Just tell me what you know."

"Don't want no coppers," said the woman. "Don't want them knowing about me."

"I won't tell the coppers about you," reassured Isabel. "Now let us in. It will be safer off the street." She nodded to Clarke. "This is my associate, Ernest Clarke. You can trust us."

Mavis appraised him and formed a favourable impression. Pastry also put on an appealing face, mainly because she could smell food. The woman was won over and let them in.

"Alfie not here?" asked Isabel as she followed the woman into a small parlour. It was clean and neat, with a sofa and two easy chairs and well maintained.

"Alfie don't live here, Miss," replied Mavis. "He'd like to, but he ain't my sort. He drinks too much for a start." She took a tin from off the small dining table. "Can the dog have a biscuit? She's so cute."

"Yes, but only one," said Isabel. "I have to watch her weight."

Mavis took great delight in giving the grateful pug a digestive, which Pastry happily crunched noisily, even licking up the crumbs she dropped on the carpet, as if she hadn't been fed for weeks. Isabel's ploy had worked. The woman had accepted them.

They sat down.

"Right," began Isabel. "As I said, I know what happens at Morgan's Meats. What happens next?"

"I went to that restaurant like the man said. I rang the bell on the side gate. It was easy. Some man gave me the meat all wrapped up. Said I could have the first bit for free. But when I walked back down the alley, these two men stopped me. They said I'd stolen the meat. I said I hadn't, but they took me inside the front of the restaurant. They searched my bag and found it. When they unwrapped the outside paper there was a label, The Silver Platter. I told them what had happened, but they said they didn't know a Derek Sparrow and someone had reported a woman hanging around the kitchens. They threatened to call the police, unless I did what they said. I was scared. Don't want no trouble."

"I see," said Isabel. "What did they want you to do?"

"They took me into see Mr Sampras. He owns the restaurant. He said he would overlook the theft, if I worked for him. I said I already had a job in the munitions, but he said he wanted me to work evenings. I could fit it in with my shifts."

"What sort of work?"

"He has this club in Soho. Got a posh French name, Le something Blanc."

"Le Chat Blanc?" queried Isabel.

"Yes, that's it."

Isabel looked at Clarke.

"The White Cat!"

"Is that what it means?" said Mavis. "Old Sampras has a white cat. Has it with him all the time. It's a mean looking thing, just like him."

"What does he look like?"

"He's fat and ugly with a big nose. Always smokes a cigar and wears lots of rings."

"So you went to work for him?" continued Isabel.

"I had no choice. At first I said I wouldn't, then they got nasty. Said they knew where I lived. I got a little kiddie, see. She's at school just now. Ma lives here, too, so looks after her when I'm out. Ma's out doing washing at the laundry. It helps now I ain't got a job."

"Do you have a husband?" asked Isabel.

"Did," replied Mavis. "He was killed last year. It's just me, the kiddie and Ma, now."

"What was your job at the club?" asked Clarke, smiling reassuringly at the woman.

"At the back of the nightclub, Sampras has a casino. It's all decked out oriental. He dresses us girls in kimonos. That's why he likes us canaries. We have yellow faces. He has all sorts of gaming going on. And the roulette wheel is fixed, so only those in the know win much. Our job was to keep the customers happy. It was men only of course. Whatever they wanted, we had to supply it.

Even…" she looked suddenly embarrassed, glancing at Clarke. "It's awkward."

"Quite," said Isabel. "I understand."

"And they do opium," added Mavis. "He has a special room for that. The state of some of them, when they're done smoking it. Like sleep walkers."

Isabel frowned. It sounded a thoroughly reprehensible organisation, with every vice readily available.

"Does he only employ munitions girls?"

"No. Anyone young and pretty will do."

"And did he find them all at the butchers?" asked Clarke.

Mavis shook her head.

"Don't know."

"Is this where you met Giles Chichester?" said Isabel.

Mavis nodded.

"He came to the club quite often with his fiancée. Sometimes, he came into the casino if he was with a group of friends and could make an excuse to leave her. He'd always been friendly. I was usually the one, who looked after him. Then, on the last night I saw him, he started asking me questions. Said he was writing some article and wanted information about Mr Sampras. I said I couldn't talk at the club. So he took out his notebook and wrote down my address. That's all. I heard someone killed him later that night."

"Did someone from the club see you talking to him?"

"Yeah, one of the croupiers told Mr Sampras's son Theo. He's Derek Sparrow by the way."

"Did he tell him straight away?"

"No, it was at the end of the night, when they were cashing up. About five o'clock."

When Chichester was already *dead*, thought Isabel.

"He got his bruisers to beat me. The croupier had seen Mr Chichester writing in his note book. I told them I ain't said anything and, eventually, they did believe me." She held up her hands. "But not before they did this."

"Have you seen a doctor?" asked Isabel.

"Can't afford a good one," said Mavis.

Isabel took out her purse and removed a £5 note. She would charge the expense to Jen-Eva Howard. She gave it to a dumfounded Mavis.

"Go and see a good doctor and get those hands treated," she said. "Then you might get your old job back. You have been very brave telling me this. Hopefully, the police will be able to close Sampras down. But, rest assured, I will not give anyone your name."

Mavis was so grateful, she insisted on giving Pastry another biscuit. The pug was so excited she broke wind.

"Sorry," apologised Isabel. "That is her way of saying thank you."

They left shortly afterwards leaving Mavis with the smell and a smile on her face.

Hattie drove them back to Cartwright Gardens.

"They seem to be going to a lot of trouble at the butcher's just to procure girls," said Isabel. "I can see how they trap them by exploiting the need for good cuts of meat, but there were lots of older women in that queue, of no interest to Sampras whatsoever. Some days they must have no suitable girls queuing at all. Do you think the shop is a front for something else?"

"I took a short walk down the side street before the shop opened," said Clarke. "There's a big store room at the back. I assumed it was for meat."

Isabel sighed.

"Anyway, I'm afraid we are back to the beginning. It sounds as if Chichester was killed before Sampras found out about Mavis Higgins. Then again, someone may have still followed him. The white cat fits."

"Pity we can't check out Chichester's rooms," said Clarke. "See if there is anything the police have missed. But, if we do, and Perch finds out, he's threatened to arrest you."

"Hmm, maybe he won't find out," replied Isabel, "if we're clever. Take a detour to Russell

Square, Hattie. Let's see if Miss Howard is at home."

Jen-Eva was, although her friend Margaret Dunstan was speaking at a meeting of women workers. She invited them inside.

"I'm afraid I cannot offer you any refreshments, as I have to go and join Margaret shortly," explained Miss Howard, making a big fuss of Pastry.

"Not a problem," replied Isabel.

"How can I help?" asked Jen-Eva.

Isabel advised the woman of what she had discovered.

"And now I am not certain what Giles was working on has any connection with his death. It would be helpful if I could take a look in his apartment, see if there is anything else in his papers. But I have to be careful as Sergeant Perch has forbidden me to interfere in his investigation, and visiting his scene of crime might constitute that. He wasn't interested in the Derek Sparrow case, so I was free to look into that. Do you, by any chance, have a key? If I can let myself in without applying to the caretaker, he may not find out I have been there."

"Yes," replied Jen-Eva. "I'll just get it for you. Giles had given me a key, so I could use his flat any time, if it was more convenient than travelling back here."

Moments later she returned with 2 keys on a ring.

"This one opens the main door," she explained, "and this the door to the apartment. It's on the ground floor, number 2."

"Excellent," said Isabel. "I will return them this evening."

"I shall be out, I'm afraid. Just post them through my letter box in an envelope or something."

"Certainly," replied Miss Hewitt. "And thank you very much."

Upon returning to Cartwright Gardens, Isabel immediately changed into her WEC uniform. She told Clarke to wear his uniform also.

"Armed with the keys, we could be visiting anyone in the building," she said. "And Perch doesn't know I'm in the WEC, so if anyone does see us and tells him, he won't think anything of it. And bring your camera. We might be able to get a helpful photograph."

Clarke had a new Autographic Vest Pocket Camera, which he planned to take back to the Western Front, when he was declared fit. Other soldiers had them although the military had not approved of the men taking their own photographs of the war. Some had found their way into the newspapers. The cameras were small, fitting into a pocket. They took 6 exposures of about 2"x 3" on a 127 film.

Hattie drove them to Stanhope Street and parked just along the road from the address. She remained in the car with Pastry, as Isabel and Clarke walked casually down the pavement. The main door to the building was not locked. There appeared to be no one about in the hallway, certainly no police. They walked along the hall to the flat. Isabel unlocked the door. Clarke examined the lock.

"No signs of the door being forced," he said.

Inside, a small hallway led down to a sitting room. It was beautifully furnished with expensive wall to wall carpets. It was decorated in an oriental style, but there was an air of masculinity about the place. Isabel looked down at the floor. The blood stains were still visible on the carpet, although someone had cleaned up. The blood spray was all over the wall and the leather furniture. Then the attack had been savage. There was a Persian rug in front of the sofa. This was stained with blood also. Isabel stood and surveyed the room. Chichester had been attacked from behind, so must have had his back to his assailant. He must have been facing the window. Had he let them in, or were they already hiding here? She looked along by the wall to see where an intruder might have hidden. Suddenly her eye was caught by four indentation marks in the carpet.

"Just a minute," she said. She walked over to the marks, bending down and putting a gloved finger in one of them. "Look at this, something heavy stood here and recently. Has it been moved?"

Clarke examined the carpet, and then looked round.

"There," he said, pointing to a medium sized, highly carved cabinet, with an enamelled front, standing near the door. "And it should have some blood splashes on it, if it stood there during the attack. See, the spray above it on the wall."

The cabinet looked clean, although someone may have wiped it down.

And it looks out of place thought Isabel. I personally wouldn't put it there. It's far too close to the door. It could easily get knocked and damaged.

Clarke walked over and examined the top.

"Dried blood on here," he said, "on either side."

"Move it," said Isabel. "Looks like our murderer did."

Clarke pulled the cabinet to one side. On the wall behind was a clear blood stained hand print.

CHAPTER EIGHT

Isabel held her gloved hand up beside the hand print on the wall.

"Well, well. This is hardly bigger than mine."

"A woman's do you think?" suggested Clarke.

"Or a man's with small hands," said Isabel, recalling Jack Forbes. She looked round. "I'll wager the murderer tripped over that rug in his haste to get away." She stood up. "I doubt it belongs to one of Sampras's bruisers. I can't imagine any of *them* being petit. It's looking less likely that this has anything to do with them. There's blood on the door handle too."

Clarke removed his camera from his pocket.

"I'll see if I can get a picture."

"Is there enough light?" asked Isabel, looking round at the window. The curtains were pulled back and, as they faced west, some late afternoon spring sunshine shone through. She stood to one side, so as not to block the light.

Clarke knelt down, extended the bellows on the little camera, set the exposure and clicked the shutter.

"I have one left," he said. Isabel knelt down again and placed her hand beside the print.

"Take one with mine for comparison."

"We need to tell the police this," said Clarke.

"And get me arrested?" replied Isabel. "Let your friend know by all means, but keep me out of it."

They replaced the cabinet. They had another look round, but, as there was nothing more of interest, they left the apartment. Isabel put the keys in the envelope she had brought with her.

"Looks as if we need to consider Chichester's jilted fiancé now," she said, "just in case our murderer is a woman. We also need to speak to the milk cart driver. I'm sure he must be able to distinguish a man from a woman, even in the dark."

They drove home via Russell Square and posted the keys through Jenna-Eva's door. Debris from the bomb blast was still being cleared.

"I won't tell her what we've found," said Isabel. "I want to be certain of my facts first."

Mrs Rhodes had cooked the fillet steak for dinner.

"That's the best piece of meat I've had in a long time," said Clarke.

Isabel agreed, amazed that such superior meat was readily available in large quantities to the Highbury butcher.

There's definitely more to this, she thought.

She planned to visit the office of *Dyke's Progress* the following morning, but, just before she was about to leave, Clarke telephoned to say she and Hattie were needed to drive ambulances. New consignments of casualties were due into Waterloo at 12 noon.

"We're to take ours to a newly opened hospital near the Arsenal football ground," he explained.

"Really?" replied Isabel.

That's convenient she thought, although she guessed that Clarke may have contrived to get the assignment. I wonder what happens at Morgan's Meats when the shop closes? By the time we get there, the shop should be shut. May be we can take a look on the way back.

The mounting numbers of the seriously injured meant that existing military hospitals were overstretched. A public hall opposite the Arsenal Football Ground had been taken over and 30 beds installed with medical staff, and the facility to do surgery if required. Hattie was to take additional casualties to the same address. Isabel changed into her WEC uniform and left immediately with her maid. Mrs Rhodes made them both some sandwiches to eat, after they arrived at the hospital.

Isabel drove with the usual care through London. She was in a convoy with six other ambulances. Upon arrival, Clarke was required to attend to his two casualties and take them inside the hospital.

"I might be a while," he said.

"Don't worry," replied Isabel "I'm sure Hattie and I will find something to do."

After eating the sandwiches, Isabel suggested they take a short walk. It was a fine spring day and Gillespie Road was busy with travellers hurrying from the tube, local residents and soldiers home on leave. They strolled down past the row of terraced houses with some of the occupants sitting out on their steps and talking to neighbours. They mingled with other people in khaki. When they came to the junction of Blackstock Road, Isabel paused. Morgan's Meats was closed and the blinds were down, but the little, wizened Chinese man, who had been helping cut up the meat, stood outside on the pavement, smoking a cigarette. She looked down the road running at the side of the shop. There were two more Chinese men standing down there, as if waiting for someone. There was no sign of Bob Morgan.

"Rather a lot of China men," said Hattie.

Isabel nodded. Did they all work for Morgan or, more likely, Theo Sampras? And why were they here if the shop was closed. Then it struck her. It must be opium. It was smoked at the White Cat Club.

I'll wager Bert Morgan is letting them use the rear of his premises for activity related to opium preparation, in return for his superior meat supply, she thought. Sampras had to keep his supplies of opium somewhere. Who would expect to find such a place in Highbury, behind an unprepossessing, little butcher's shop? No wonder they used such violence on Mavis Higgins. They were protecting their drugs racket. The procuring of the girls was an added bonus. But, if it was some kind of opium den, that was a matter for the police. Then she had another uncomfortable thought. The wizened Chinese man was quite small in stature. Did he have *small* hands? She tried to remember, but she hadn't taken that much notice of him. Even so, the pendulum was swinging back to the Sampras operation.

I have to speak to that milk cart driver, she thought. Would he be able to tell if the man, who collided with his horse, was Chinese?

After Clarke had finished his work at the newly installed hospital, Isabel drove him back in convoy to the ambulance depot with Hattie following behind. All three had finished work for the afternoon.

"I'd like to visit Fred Ames, now," said Isabel. She had explained to Clarke, on the way back, what she saw in Blackstock Road. "And I think you should have a word with Tom about that place."

"I will," he said. "I don't want *you* getting involved with anything like that. I'll meet him tonight."

I'll try not to, thought Isabel.

They drove back to Cartwright Gardens and collected Fred Ames' address. Isabel decided to take Pastry with her. Mrs Rhodes had been looking after the pug nearly all day. Hattie stayed behind to help the housekeeper. Clarke drove to Camden. Fred Ames was at home. He was an amiable man in his fifties. His wife was equally amiable and very taken with Pastry. Fred sat smoking a pipe by the fireplace and drinking a mug of very strong tea. Mrs Ames offered them tea, also, but Isabel politely declined. She explained who she was and why she was calling. He was impressed by their uniforms.

"I told that Sergeant Perch all I saw," he said.

"I realise that," replied Isabel, "and I know it was dark, but did you see the man's face? Was he Chinese by any chance?"

"No, definitely not," said Ames, "though he had his hair in some kind of pigtail, pulled back. I saw it when his cap fell off. He was definitely white."

"And he ran into your horse?"

"Came out of nowhere, he did. Right spooked my old Nancy. He was covered in blood too. It was smeared all over her flanks. But he copped it when she kicked his knee. Ran off limping he did. Hope they get the blighter. My Nancy is still a bit nervous. Not usually many folk about that time of the morning."

"You are certain he was a man?" asked Isabel.

The man's face creased with a puzzled frown.

"What do you mean?"

"Could he have been a woman dressed as a man?"

"A *woman*?" The man considered. "You mean like them male impersonators in the Music Hall?"

"Yes," said Isabel.

Fred Ames sucked on his pipe.

"Don't reckon he had a beard or a moustache. But a woman? Why dress like a man at that time of night?"

"A disguise?" suggested Isabel.

The man nodded.

"True, but I can't be sure, Miss. My Nancy was real spooked. It took me all my time to get her under control."

"Of course. Thank you Mr Ames, you've been very helpful."

At least he was certain of one thing. The man running away from the apartment, covered in blood, was not Chinese.

Clarke drove Isabel back to Cartwright Gardens. It would appear the focus of their investigation must switch back to elements in Chichester's personal life. Isabel telephoned Hugh and asked if he would accompany her to the office of *Dyke's Progress* the next day.

After another sumptuous meal of rump steak this time, Clarke went to meet his friend Tom Barry.

"Don't mention the handprint just yet," said Isabel. "I don't want Perch blundering in and accusing anyone. I need to be sure of my ground."

And she didn't want to be arrested either. If only Mangle would return. She would definitely have told him.

Clarke came back later that evening and, with him, he brought the small photographs from his camera. Someone had processed them for him at the hospital.

"They came out all right," he said, showing them to Isabel. Miss Hewitt saw he had four other pictures. One looked like Clarke with a dog.

"What about those?" she asked. "Is that you with a dog?"

He looked suddenly sheepish.

"Erm, yes. That's Tucker. Actually he's mine."

"*Your* dog?" said Isabel.

"Yes, he was a stray hanging round the hospital. The police wanted to shoot him, but I decided I would save him. He's a lurcher. He's being trained at the moment as a Mercy Dog. The breed is very good for searching out the wounded on the battlefield." He paused. "I hope to take him with me when I go back to the Front. We can work together."

Isabel nodded and tried to hide the sudden chill that seized her. It was a salutary reminder. She had become used to Clarke being at home and working as an orderly. But, as a private in the Royal Medical Core, he must eventually return to the theatre of death. He was making preparations already. She had no choice but accept it.

He showed her the other photographs of Tucker. He looked an intelligent, bright eyed dog and very hairy, just the sort to have fleas. But, she assumed, that would have been taken care of.

"You must bring him here," she said. "I would like to meet him."

"What about Pastry?" asked Clarke.

"I'm sure she would like to meet him, too," replied Isabel. Pastry was currently snoring in her basket and, as no one had any food, was not taking much interest in the conversation!

"Did you tell Tom about Morgan's Meats?" she asked changing the shift of the conversation.

"Yes, I did," he said. "Apparently Inspector Mangle is working on something similar. Tom said he would pass the information on."

"So if we've helped him, we might get Mangle back on the Chichester case," said Isabel. "I shall look forward to that."

CHAPTER NINE

The following morning Hattie drove Isabel to Hugh's office and then on to New Fetter Lane.

"I did inform them we were planning to call again," he said. "Let's hope Hilliard has found his manners this time."

They found the office more or less how they had left it on the previous visit. Andrew Hilliard was busy checking text, Jack Forbes was finishing off a cartoon and Alice Colman typed industriously.

"Please be brief, Miss Hewitt," said Hilliard with hardly a glance at her. "I have a magazine to put together."

Once again Jack Forbes offered Isabel a seat. She glanced at his small hands as he pulled the chair towards her. Were they similar in size to the blood stained print? She noted his hair tied back in a pigtail, but she was not aware of a limp. Surely a kick from Fred Ames' mare would still be painful. Was he Amelia Hilliard's champion? Had he brutally stabbed Giles Chichester that night?

"Very well," she began, sitting down. "It has come to my notice that the murderer of your friend, Giles Chichester, may well have been female."

Hilliard immediately looked up.

"What? How do you know?"

"I am not at liberty to divulge that," replied Isabel cagily, "but, as your sister is his jilted fiancée, and would have reasonable grounds for revenge, I feel I ought to speak with her, just to clarify her situation. Therefore, I would like her address. I believe she is residing in Eastbourne."

"No, out of the question," replied Hilliard. "Amelia would never do such a thing! Never!"

"I would be very discreet," reassured Isabel. "It would be just for elimination purposes."

"I said no," repeated Hilliard. "My sister is suffering badly with her nerves. All this business with Giles has quite disconcerted her. She has had to move back to London, as sometimes, down on the coast, she could hear the distant sound of the guns booming on the continent. We have a brother fighting out in Belgium. It was too much for her to bear, the thought that one of them might be killing him."

Isabel nodded and felt the same chill ripple through her body, as when Clarke told her about Tucker and his return to the Front.

"I sympathise. That must have been very unpleasant for her. And I would certainly bear that in mind. But, unfortunately, I feel I still need to speak with her."

Hilliard suddenly boiled over with anger.

"Just who do you think you are, Miss Hewitt? Just because Jen-Eva Howard takes it upon herself to hire you to investigate Giles's death, it doesn't give you the right to harass my family. I forbid you to go anywhere near my sister. I gather Sergeant Perch has told you as much, too. This case is in the hands of the police and that is where it should stay."

"Now hold on, Hilliard," blustered Hugh.

Isabel put a restraining hand on his arm.

"I see your animosity towards Miss Howard is still clouding your judgment, Mr Hilliard." Isabel stood up. "In that case, I have no alternative but to pass this information over to Sergeant Perch. He does not know about it yet. His interviewing technique is, perhaps, a little more direct than mine and the experience might be more traumatic for your sister. But that is your choice" She placed her business card down on Jack Forbes' desk. "However, if you change your mind, or if Miss Hilliard chooses to see me, I can be contacted at this address. Good day to you."

She swept out of the office again, before anyone could reply and walked back to the car in silence.

"What now?" said Hugh, as they climbed inside.

"We wait," replied Isabel. "I am hoping Amelia Hilliard is not the docile, neurotic woman her brother thinks she is and Jack Forbes will be keen to help her. With any luck he will bring her to my house and I can speak to them both. Jack Forbes is a possible suspect too. It is the sensible thing to do. By keeping quiet they cast suspicion on themselves, now they know there is evidence pointing to a woman killer. Amelia Hilliard, more than anyone, has a creditable motive."

They dropped Hugh back at his office and drove back to Cartwright Gardens. After lunch, Isabel planned to visit the theatrical costumier to return the wig. As she was about to leave, she received a visitor. Hattie ushered a very self-assured Miss Amelia Hilliard into the sitting room. She was a pretty, young woman with blonde curls, expertly coiffured and wore a smart, stylish dress, with matching jacket. She oozed elegance and style, with just enough make up to enhance the impression of a lady and her fingernails were equally, expertly manicured. Isabel had difficulty in imagining her dressed as a man with cloth cap. In fact she totally approved of her appearance. Pastry barked at once and ran across to greet the visitor.

"What a lovely little dog," exclaimed Miss Hilliard, scooping Pastry into her arms and giving her a suffocating hug. "Can you smell my Ruggles?" The pug, at once, felt uncomfortable being smothered by a perfect stranger and began to wriggle. Isabel rescued her and declined to enquire what Miss Hilliard meant by her Ruggles.

"Miss Hilliard, do come in and have a seat."

Amelia sat down.

"I am sorry to call unannounced," she said. "But Jack telephoned and I felt I just had to clear my name as soon as possible. He said you suspect Giles' killer might be a woman."

"Indeed," replied Isabel. "And thank you for responding so quickly."

She sat down on the chesterfield and placed Pastry on her lap.

"May I offer you some tea?"

Her visitor fussily rearranged the folds of her skirt.

"No thank you, Miss Hewitt. I have an appointment with my hairdresser in half an hour. But to business, firstly I gather my brother has been rather rude to you. It's not personal you understand, it's because you are working on behalf of Jen-Eva Howard. Andy just can't abide her. Even when Giles was alive, she kept trying to interfere with the magazine. I hope you haven't taken offence."

"Not at all," replied Isabel.

"I gather Jen-Eva is quite a domineering sort of woman, not Giles' kind at all. He did like to control people. He must have found her quite a challenge."

"You found him controlling?" asked Isabel.

Amelia sighed.

"Yes I did and, to tell you the truth, I was getting tired of it. But he had this roguish charm you see and could be quite irresistible when he wanted."

"Can you tell me where you were on the night Giles was killed?" asked Isabel, getting to the point.

"Certainly. I was in Eastbourne, dancing at a rather good nightclub actually." She pulled a small business card from her bag. "Here is the name of the club." She turned the card over. "And this is the name of a friend Jonathan Russell, who is a member there. You can check it all with him, or the police can if they so wish."

"Were you with Mr Russell that night?"

"Yes, I was with a group of his friends. Actually I was partnered by Jack Forbes. We have been seeing each other for about two months now. When Giles jilted me, I was naturally devastated.

Jack was so supportive. Our friendship grew from there." She paused. "Jack doesn't want Andy to know yet, in case he disapproves and sacks him. But what I do is none of Andy's business. Jack says you said you would be discreet. You won't tell Andy will you?"

My two mains suspects out of the equation in one stroke thought Isabel, provided, of course, Miss Hilliard spoke the truth. The account of her whereabouts that night was very well documented. No doubt Mr Russell would corroborate everything. Was it too good to be true?

"No, of course not, "she replied. "That is your place to do that."

"Actually I have returned to London to tell Andy about it. I think it's time he knew. Jack has asked me to marry him."

"Your brother claimed you came back because you could hear the guns booming on the Front and it upset you."

Amelia pulled a pained face.

"Yes, you can hear them faintly, but only when the wind is in the right direction. It is upsetting when you have family out there, but it doesn't happen that often. My brother gets some funny ideas into his head sometimes. I think he regards me as some kind of highly strung child. I told him about the guns and he just assumed the rest. I love Eastbourne and plan to go back there."

"So you had no hard feelings towards Giles Chichester now?"

"No, although I'm sorry someone has murdered him naturally, Miss Hewitt. But it definitely wasn't anything to do with me. It is over six months since we were together. Surely, if I had wanted some kind of retribution, I would have murdered him then, not now. And," she paused, "surely I would have wanted *her* out of the way not him. *She* was my rival. I would have murdered *her*."

Isabel nodded. That made some sort of sense.

"So, who do you think might want Giles dead?" she asked.

"Giles was a gambling man, Miss Hewitt. And the work he did upset people. It could be anyone.

But I suggest you look closer at Miss Howard and her circle. Perhaps, someone there saw Giles as a rival."

"Indeed," said Isabel. "That thought had not occurred to me. Do you suggest anyone in particular?"

Her visitor shrugged.

"I am not familiar with Miss Howard's acquaintances, except for that secretary of hers."

"You mean Miss Dunstan?"

"Is that her name? Andy described her as excessively dreary. A champion of women's rights I believe. I've never needed one."

Then you don't work for a living thought Isabel.

But was Amelia Hilliard trying to point the finger at Margaret Dunstan? It seemed all rather convenient, along with the seemingly cast iron account of where she was on the night of the murder. Isabel had to ensure she wasn't being duped. The lady seemed quite capable of that. Pastry suddenly barked on her lap, making them both jump.

"I'm sorry," apologised Isabel, seizing an opportunity for a vital question. "Dogs can be noisy at times. I might be better off with a cat. Do you have any pets Miss Hilliard?"

"I have a King Charles spaniel, my darling Ruggles," replied Amelia. "And I loathe cats. They bring me out in unsightly spots."

"So, Jack doesn't have a cat then?"

"No, the poor dear couldn't afford it; he gets paid so little by my miserly brother. But he does prefer dogs anyway."

There was little more to ask Miss Hilliard and the lady soon made her excuses to leave, so as not to be late for her hairdresser, although her hair looked in immaculate condition. She left Isabel with much to ponder. She hadn't given Margaret Dunstan a second thought and knew relatively nothing about her. But what possible motive could she have? She was just an employee of Miss Howard's. But, in the absence of anyone else, she would see what she could discover, although she planned to keep an open mind about Miss Hilliard and Jack Forbes. She would seek Clarke's opinion at the first available opportunity.

Miss Hewitt Investigates the White Cat

CHAPTER TEN

Hattie drove Isabel to the theatrical costumier, but, on their return to Cartwright Gardens, they found another unexpected visitor waiting to see Miss Hewitt. Alice Colman sat nervously in the sitting room.

Isabel smiled reassuringly at her guest.

"Miss Colman, good afternoon. Has anyone offered you tea?"

Alice nodded.

"Yes, your housekeeper did, but I said no. I wasn't sure if I would be welcome."

It was obvious the girl was slightly afraid of Isabel, probably because she had seen her in full flow with Andrew Hilliard and was fearful she might get the same, short treatment.

"Nonsense," replied Isabel. "You are very welcome and I insist we have some now." She looked at Hattie. "Tell Mrs Rhodes we will take tea for two."

"Yes, Ma'am," replied Hattie, who still held a wriggly Pastry in her arms. "I'll take the dog to the kitchen too. I think it's time for her dinner."

"Now," said Isabel, sitting down opposite Alice Colman. "What can I do for you?"

It wasn't immediately clear why the girl had called to see her. But Isabel felt it had to be important.

Alice pulled a sheet of paper from her bag.

"Mr Forbes reckoned I should call round and show you this?" She handed it over. "It's an article Mr Chichester was going to publish in the magazine. I typed it ready, but then he was murdered before he could submit it to Mr Hilliard."

Isabel looked at the paper. The title ran:

CHAMPION OF WOMEN'S RIGHTS OR JUST JEALOUS OF MEN?

The article was a scathing attack on Margaret Dunstan. It accused her of being a lesbian and a frequenter of a property in Soho called The Golden Lion, where women of the same persuasion could meet, dress in men's clothes and indulge in, what Chichester described as, their misguided lusts. It inferred, as the title suggested, an envy of men by a group of pathetic women. And put an unfavourable slant on Dunstan's reasons for championing women's rights. Isabel found it quite damning in tone and grossly unfair.

"Is any of this true?" she asked.

"I don't know, Miss," replied Alice. "I only type up Mr Chichester's notes. But I know he had it in for Miss Dunstan. He didn't like the influence she had over Miss Howard."

And this was his way of getting control of her, thought Isabel, the swine. Had the article been published, Miss Dunstan's reputation would be in tatters, even if it wasn't true. She would have the indignity of trying to disprove it. It would leave Jen-Eva Howard with no choice but to dispense with Dunstan's services to avoid a scandal, although Isabel felt what Miss Dunstan did in her private life was no one else's business. But people with a public life had to tread a fine line of respectability, unless you were like the generous and big hearted Marie Lloyd, whose public forgave her everything. The initial public disgrace would remove Dunstan's influence on Jen-Eva, which was exactly what Chichester wanted.

I really despise this man, she thought.

"Did Miss Dunstan know what he was planning?" she asked instead.

The secretary nodded.

"He said she saw him spying on her at the Golden Lion. He gloated about the way he managed to get into such an exclusive place. It wouldn't surprise me if he did tell her what he was going to do. He could be spiteful like that."

"Had he told Miss Howard?" Even as she asked the question, Isabel could guess the answer. Jen-Eva knew nothing about it. This despicable Chichester character wanted her to *read* about it in his nasty little magazine.

But this gave Margaret Dunstan a genuine motive for murder. And she had access to keys to Chichester's apartment. It was all rather disquieting.

"May I keep this for the time being?" she asked, nodding to the article.

"Yes, Miss," replied Alice. "Mr Forbes told me to type you a copy."

"Who else knows about these accusations?"

"Only Mr Forbes, Miss and me. It never got as far as Mr Hilliard. I think Jack planned to throw the article away, but when you suggested the murderer might be a woman, he wanted to protect Miss Amelia. That's why he told me to show it to you."

Everyone wants to protect Miss Hilliard thought Isabel, and the lady is quite able to look after herself.

But Margaret Dunstan was different. She was an intense character, who took herself very seriously and, Isabel felt, was quite sincere in her beliefs in championing women's rights. She would be quite vulnerable to a divisive predator like Chichester, particularly if she was a lesbian. And what did that say about her feelings for Jen-Eva?

I need to speak to her she thought, just to see the lie of the land.

"Do you have any idea where Miss Dunstan lives?" she asked. "Is it with Miss Howard in Russell Square?"

"No Miss," replied Alice. "Mr Chichester said she still lived with her parents in Tavistock Place. The address is at the bottom of the page, although she was angling to move in with Miss Howard."

And he wanted to prevent that at all costs thought Isabel.

At this point, Hattie arrived with the tea.

After Alice Colman left, Isabel read the article again. Could this spiteful piece be true? If not, Margaret Dunstan could sue him for libel? But that would take time and the initial damage would have been done. Isabel had never heard of the Golden Lion, but she knew someone who might have. Elvira Stone was a wealthy, eccentric woman, who made no secret of that fact she was a lesbian. Isabel had known her since she was a child. Elvira's father was the Colonel of Isabel's father's regiment in India. About 16 years Isabel's senior, she had often played with the officers' young children and, after both their fathers died of enteric fever in the Boer war, Isabel had kept in touch. In fact Elvira had been a great support at that difficult time. The woman was erudite, well-travelled and always spoke her mind. She spent her life painting mostly unremarkable oils of foreign landscapes, which she often gave away to friends, although if anyone was predisposed to buy, she would take their money. Isabel had two of these paintings, which were currently gathering dust in her attic. Elvira lived alone in a rambling old house in Bayswater, although her door was always open to any girls, who needed a place to stay. She'd had a long term lover once, but she had died a few years ago.

Hattie drove Isabel to the address. Elvira opened the front door and was delighted to see her and Pastry standing on her doorstep.

"Little Izzie!" she exclaimed. "This is a lovely surprise, and you've brought little 'stinky bottom', too. Come in. Come in." She was a big woman with dark red, wiry hair, pinned back in a haphazard bun and a big, rosy cheeked, friendly face. She had a fondness for Pastry, whom she affectionately referred to as 'Stinky Bottom'. She wore a dark man's suit, almost completely covered in flecks of paint down the front. Elvira always wore it when painting. "I'm in the studio," she explained. "You don't mind do you?"

"Not all," replied Isabel.

Elvira led her guest through to the back of the rambling house and into her chaotic studio. Finished paintings leaned against the walls, whilst countless copies of the Daily Express and empty paint pots were strewn everywhere. Elvira could never be bothered to throw anything away. Pots of brushes stood on a filthy side table together with a palette of mixed paints. On an easel in the centre of the room stood the painting Elvira currently worked on.

"Corfu," she explained. "I was there in 09. Last place I went with Phyllis." Isabel nodded. Elvira had told her that before. "Now, sit yourself down." Elvira pointed to some easy chairs at the far end of the room, arranged around a small table, on which stood a sherry decanter and some glasses. It was the only area of the studio that appeared clean. "And let little 'Stinky Bottom' have a bit of a play. He can't do any harm. And you must let him sit for me. He has the most charming little face." He's a she thought Isabel. She'd told Elvira that many times, but the woman never remembered. She decided to keep hold of Pastry for the time being. The pug found Miss Stone rather overwhelming and preferred the safety of Isabel's lap. But the experience prompted a wind, which amused her host. "Not changed has he? Fancy a sherry? How's that manservant of yours? Still living with you?"

She poured two generous sherries and handed one to Isabel, before Miss Hewitt could draw breath to answer.

"I think he may be returning to the Front soon," she replied eventually, as she sat down and her host did likewise.

Elvira's mood immediately sobered.

"Yes. That ghastly business. I thought the Boer one was bad enough. But the carnage in this one is dreadful, what with all the names of those poor chaps in the paper." She downed her sherry in one gulp and poured another. "Now Izzie, is this just a social call, or are you engaged in one of your little detective jobs?"

"I'm afraid it is the latter," explained Isabel with a smile. "A name has come to my notice. Are you familiar with the Golden Lion in Soho? Is it what used to be termed a Molly House, but for women?"

Elvira was surprised.

"Good Lord Izzie, what do you want to know about that for?" She paused. "Of course, it's information for your case eh?" She leaned forward and picked up a packet of cheroots from the floor. She took one out and lit up with a gold plated lighter. "Yes, it is what used to be known as a Molly house. It's a club where lesbians can go and meet like-minded women." She exhaled the smoke. "What we do is not illegal, not like the chaps. But some feel the need to be inconspicuous. Martha Green runs the place. Very discreet, she is. Downstairs, it's just a bar, but out the back there is a room set aside. That's for women members only and everyone is vetted before they can join. It's a place to meet, socialise, dress up and do whatever you like. You'd be surprised who goes there, but there anonymity is preserved. Martha is very particular about that. It's a while since I went. Don't have the need now, but I keep in touch with the place."

"Do you know if a Margaret Dunstan goes there?"

"Dunstan?" Elvira thought for a moment. "You mean the Dunstan, who champions women's rights?" Isabel nodded. Elvira shook her head. "I've not heard she's a member. She works for that smug female Jen-Eva Howard doesn't she? Can't imagine *her* wanting a lesbian in her employ." She took another long draw on the cheroot. "I heard Margaret Dunstan speak at a meeting once. I was really impressed. She was very passionate and convincing. I met her afterwards and could hardly get a word out of her. She was very restrained, buttoned right up I'd say. That Howard woman had far too much to say, though." Elvira suddenly looked directly at Isabel. "She was engaged to that Giles Chichester. You're not caught up in all that murder business are you?"

"I can't possible say," replied Isabel.

"That means you are." Elvira frowned. "He came snooping round here once, trying to dig up some scandal on me, the poisonous little runt. I sent him packing." She laughed. "I tried to sell him one of my paintings!"

"I didn't know the man," replied Isabel. "But what I've found out suggests a thoroughly despicable type."

"Yes," said Elvira. "His family are in sweets, but there was nothing sweet about him. Too cowardly to fight for King and country, he preferred using his pen to try and assassinate people. I told him as much too. He didn't like it. Is Margaret Dunstan mixed up in all this?"

"I don't know," replied Isabel cagily. "At the moment her only involvement is as Miss Howard's secretary. As I said the Golden Lion name has just cropped up."

"Hmm." Elvira decided not to probe, but guessed Dunstan's name had been linked with the place or why would Isabel inquire. She changed the subject. "Now you must let me do a sketch of 'Stinky Bottom' whilst you are here. Let's go through to the sitting room. I have my drawing pad there."

After Isabel left, Elvira found herself facing a dilemma. She hadn't been totally truthful about Margaret Dunstan. The woman was a regular at the Golden Lion and, in fact, Elvira had shared some passionate moments with her. She knew Margaret detested Chichester and, sadly, had an unrequited love for Jen-Eva Howard. But, if she was caught up in this business, and Isabel was on her tail, she should be very afraid. Should she warn her? But that would mean she would betray one of her dearest friends, who was almost like family to her. She was also proud of Isabel's formidable reputation as a detective. For once in her life, Elvira Stone decided to say nothing and just hoped Margaret Dunstan hadn't done anything stupid.

CHAPTER ELEVEN

That evening, Isabel discussed the developments with Clarke. He found the article disturbing.

"But there is no actual evidence to link the murder to Margaret Dunstan," he said. "This piece was never published. We don't even know if she was aware of it."

"There is the hand print on the wall," suggested Isabel. "If that is found to match Margaret Dunstan's hand, then the police will have all they need."

"They will have to get her finger prints first. And what reason can they have to ask her?"

"That's true, but I can't stop thinking that it was Miss Dunstan, who pointed us in the direction of Derek Sparrow."

"Did you tell Elvira about that?"

"I didn't tell Elvira any particulars of the case, certainly not that article. I was only interested in the Golden Lion."

"But you mentioned Dunstan?"

"Yes, and she has met her at a meeting. But she said she hadn't heard she went there."

"Do you believe her?"

Isabel considered.

"I'm not sure. The patrons of that club are fiercely loyal to each other. I doubt she would betray anyone, even to me, so, perhaps, Dunstan is a member and that spiteful article has some truth in it."

"Would she warn Margaret Dunstan that you were asking about her?"

Isabel gave a wry smile.

"I'm not sure about that either. But, I plan to call on her tomorrow at home. She only lives in Tavistock Place. She will know of my interest then."

"What will you say?"

Isabel shrugged.

"I don't know; probably ask her about Jen-Eva's social circle. But I won't mention I think the killer is a woman. As far as she knows, we are still looking for a male."

"Be careful," he said. "Take Hattie with you. Dunstan may be more deranged than you think."

"I will," replied Isabel. "And I will treat her more as a witness. After all we don't *know* she is involved yet."

"She may know we went to Chichester's flat, as we borrowed Jen-Eva's keys."

"Yes, but She won't guess we moved the cabinet. The police didn't. No, I think, if she is our killer, she is confidant she is not under suspicion. But, at the moment, I cannot prove it, anyway. She is just another suspect I have to eliminate."

But, if it wasn't Dunstan, Isabel had no idea where to look next.

The following morning, Isabel was up very early. She had tried to envisage Margaret Dunstan's hair. How long was it? She hadn't taken that much notice. She felt it was pinned back in some kind of bun, so she may have been able to plait it into a pig-tail. She knew exactly what she wanted to say and decided not to take Hattie, or Dunstan's suspicions might be aroused. She wanted to be as informal as possible. But, she did put her father's revolver into her bag, just in case. Before she left, she read some good news in The Times.

'POLICE RAID HIGHBURY BUTCHER'S SHOP. LARGE QUANTITY OF OPIUM FOUND' ran the headline. Inspector Mangle had led the raid. An unnamed business man and his associates had been arrested.

Well, at least that part of the investigation was successful she thought. She couldn't help thinking Sampras hadn't been that clever. Supplying all that superior meat to such a small time butcher and procuring the girls, would have aroused someone's suspicions eventually.

It was a fine spring morning. A chaffinch sung somewhere in the trees in the gardens. She always found the song exhilarating. She strolled along to Tavistock Place and to the address Alice Colman gave her. A maid answered the door.

"Good morning," said Isabel, deliberately amiably. "Is Miss Dunstan at home?"

"Afraid not," replied the maid. "Mrs Dunstan is in, though."

"Then perhaps I could speak to her?" suggested Isabel. "My name is Miss Hewitt and this is my card."

She handed over one of her business cards. The maid gave that and Miss Hewitt the once over and decided she looked respectable. She admitted her into the hall.

"Wait here, Miss," she said.

The maid disappeared into the house, and then, moments later, came back.

"If you'd like to follow me, Miss, Mrs Dunstan will see you in the parlour."

Mrs Dunstan was a small, stout woman who looked nothing like her daughter at all. The parlour was expensively decorated and comfortably furnished. The Dunstans must have money.

"Good morning, Miss Hewitt," she said, indicating Isabel sit down. "My daughter has told me all about you. Jen-Eva has asked you to look into Giles Chichester's death."

"That is correct," replied Isabel, taking a seat opposite her host.

"Nasty business," said Mrs Dunstan, "though I didn't care for the man. He came here to dinner one evening with Jen-Eva. He was far too oleaginous for my taste. Mr Dunstan didn't take to him either, although he is very partial to the father's cream fudge." She frowned. "And Margaret told me he was always abominably rude to her, dismissed her work as if it was nothing."

"Yes, I gather he was a bit of a cad," said Isabel.

"A bit?" exclaimed Mrs Dunstan .She looked at the maid. "Bring more coffee and a cup for Miss Hewitt. You can stay for coffee I assume."

"Certainly and thank you," replied Isabel.

Mrs Dunstan sighed.

"Yes, nasty business. We were all very shocked of course and Miss Howard was devastated. That upset poor Margaret. She is a very loyal person. She's quite devoted to her, even though she is just an employee."

At this point a *white cat*, with bright blue eyes, slunk round the door frame and into the room. Isabel was taken by surprise. She hadn't expected this.

"My goodness," she exclaimed, concealing the real reason for her surprise, "is this *your* cat?"

Mrs Dunstan nodded.

"She's Margaret's actually. Her name's Sapphire on account of her lovely eyes."

The cat slunk across to Isabel, who picked her up. She stared straight into those blue eyes.

"Yes, I thought so. You and I have met before in Cartwright Gardens haven't we? My pug, Pastry, always chases you." The cat purred. Isabel sat the cat on her lap and stroked her. The fur was soft. "What a beautiful coat," she murmured. As desired, cat hairs fell onto her skirt. Her plan was working better than she had dared hope.

"Yes, she does wander about," said Mrs Dunstan, smiling. "Then, that's what cats do I suppose. She always comes home, though."

"And look at all your hair!" chuckled Isabel, nodding to her skirt. "You're almost as bad as my pug. She leaves hair everywhere, mainly in places she shouldn't."

"Yes. My apologies," replied Mrs Dunstan. "Sapphire is just the same. She even used one of my husband's favourite old caps to sleep in. It fell off the peg in the scullery one day and she just took hold of it. He used to wear it when he went out into the garden. It was one of those big ones. Sapphire curled herself right inside, quite ruined it. He refused to wear it after that. Margaret threw it out in the end."

Really, thought Isabel. I suspect it's actually at Scotland Yard. The evidence was stacking up against Margaret Dunstan.

"So, your daughter is not at home?" she asked.

"No, she left early to go to Jen-Eva's. I think that woman works her too hard. She's always been an early riser. If it's daylight, Margaret gets up. But these days she comes home late and stays up working on her speeches. Sometimes she stays out most of the night. I don't think she's getting enough sleep, but she doesn't listen to me. We're all so proud of her, although, her father doesn't agree with a lot of her politics. It does lead to harsh words at times."

"Yes, fathers and daughters," replied Isabel. "I remember having many disagreements with mine. Sadly, he's no longer with me." She looked at the woman. "So you don't expect Margaret to be home any time soon?"

"No. I doubt I will see her until just before we retire to bed. She's often out in the evenings. Lord only knows where she goes. Is there any message? Or you could try Russell Square."

"I just wanted to speak to her about Miss Howard," replied Isabel. "It would be better to speak to her alone you understand."

Mrs Dunstan nodded. At this point the maid arrived with the coffee. Isabel began to feel uncomfortable. The woman had more or less provided her damning evidence about her daughter, even though it was circumstantial. But who else owned a white cat, who slept in a cap? She ventured one more question.

"How is Margaret's knee? I heard she had a nasty fall."

"Yes, poor love. She tripped over a pavement and went right down on it. Her knee was so badly swollen she could hardly walk, but she wouldn't see a doctor. I thought she might have broken a bone, but she said it was just bruised. She can be so stubborn. We bandaged it up for her. I think it's going down a bit now. She's walking better anyway. I told her to report it. Someone else might not be so lucky, but she didn't."

That's because she was kicked by a horse thought Isabel. She decided she had heard enough, and made an excuse to leave, shortly afterwards.

"I am driving a military ambulance this afternoon," she explained, which was true.

"I'll tell Margaret you called," said Mrs Dunstan.

"Thank you," replied Isabel.

She hurried back to Cartwright Gardens with mixed emotions. Normally she didn't allow sentiment to cloud her judgement, having an unshakable belief in justice. But this time she was unsure. To obtain justice for this parasite of a man, she would have to bring down a woman, who did genuine good, who championed women's rights and who would be missed.

I can't do it, she thought. I shall just tell Perch all I know and he can decide. Oh Margaret, why did you have to do this foolish thing? Giles Chichester just wasn't worth it.

Upon her return to Cartwright Gardens, Isabel put a call through to Scotland Yard. She asked to speak to Clarke's friend, Tom Barry, but Sergeant Perch answered with an abrupt 'yes'.

"Isabel Hewitt here, Sergeant," she said. She heard him snort. "Just to let you know I have discovered something important about the murder of Giles Chichester. I know who the killer is."

He snorted again.

"What? I distinctly told you leave well alone. Andrew Hilliard told me you had been bothering his family."

"Yes, I am sorry, but my investigation has taken an unexpected twist and I need to see you urgently."

"Where are you?" he snapped.

"At home, naturally, Sergeant, but I shall be leaving around noon."

The phone was slammed down the other end.

He's on his way she thought.

She found the article and the photographs and put them beside her chair, ready to show him. She tided the room and put Pastry's piece of knotted rope under her chair. Pastry thought she was about to have a game, but when Isabel sat down and picked up the paper to read more about the opium raid, she gave up and settled down on the carpet in a shaft of sunlight. Suddenly there was a sharp knock on the front door. Pastry barked and ran to the sitting room door.

That was quick, Isabel thought. Then your ancestor was a Bow Street Runner. She glanced out of the window to make sure who the caller was. To her consternation she found it was Margaret Dunstan.

No, she thought. I am not ready for you. I must speak to Perch first or, at least have him here when I do challenge you. To accuse the woman with no witnesses present was pointless. She hurried into the hall to waylay Hattie.

"The caller is Margaret Dunstan. Please tell her I am not at home."

Hattie looked puzzled, but did not query the request. Isabel picked up Pastry and returned to the sitting room, but left the door ajar. She heard Hattie lie quite convincingly and send the caller away. Isabel was surprised to discover how tense she felt, and how relieved she was Miss Dunstan had gone. She sat down at her baby grand piano and gently fingered a soothing tune with one hand. These sudden and unexpected developments had taken her by surprise. She needed to plan in her head how she might broach the subject. Dunstan was obviously a clever woman, but she wasn't a criminal. She might be struggling, herself, with the guilt of what she had done. Suddenly Pastry, who had fallen asleep again in the shaft of sunlight, growled a warning and then barked. Isabel wheeled round and, to her dismay, saw Margaret Dunstan framed in the open doorway.

CHAPTER TWELVE

"Miss Dunstan, good morning," said Isabel, schooling her expression to disguise her disquiet. "I didn't hear you come in."

"I came through the back way," replied the woman briskly. She had a belligerent look in her eye. "Your housekeeper and maid were busy with the washing. I just came in through the kitchen. I knew you were at home, even though your maid said you weren't. I saw you at the window."

Isabel smiled ingenuously.

"How very observant of you, Miss Dunstan. Please come in and sit down. The truth is, I am expecting a visit from Sergeant Perch any minute, and feel it might be a bit stormy. I didn't want anyone else caught up in it. I didn't mean any offence."

The woman nodded and accepted the explanation. She sat down.

"Let me offer you a sherry," insisted Isabel. She moved across to the drinks cabinet, before the woman could decline, and removed two glasses. She was careful to hold Miss Dunstan's by the stem only.

So much for me not wanting to catch her out, she thought. We should get a good set of fingerprints from the glass. She gave it to her visitor. Unsuspecting, Margaret took hold of it. She frowned as she took a sip.

"My mother telephoned and told me you had called to see me. How did you find out where I lived?"

Isabel sat down opposite and casually covered the article and photographs with The Times newspaper.

"Somebody told me," she said. Fortunately, at this moment, Pastry began sniffing around Margaret Dunstan's skirt and Isabel was able to deflect the conversation by pulling the pug away. "I'm sorry. She can probably smell your lovely cat. I've seen her several times in the gardens opposite. She's quite adorable."

Miss Dunstan did not respond to the compliment and remained defensive.

She's rattled, thought Isabel. She probably knows her mother told me about the cap, too, and the knee injury and is anxious as to what I suspect.

Margaret Dunstan finished her sherry in one gulp. Isabel took the glass back from her, once again holding the stem only, and placed it on the table by her chair.

"Would you care for another?"

Dunstan shook her head.

"So, Miss Hewitt, why do you want to see me?"

Isabel smiled and sat down again.

"I'm afraid we suspect Giles Chichester's killer might be someone in Jen-Eva's circle. I just wanted to know if you had any ideas on the subject."

A flash of relief momentarily shot across Dunstan's face, and then she returned to her former defensive manner.

"I thought it was something to do with Giles's work and that man Derek Sparrow."

"I looked into that," replied Isabel. She pointed to The Times. "We unearthed an opium den, which the police have just raided. But, I am satisfied Giles's death is nothing to do with that operation. I suspect it is a bit closer to home." She gave her guest a level glance. "So, any ideas?"

Margaret was suddenly uneasy.

"No, I can't think of anyone."

Then I shall suggest you leave thought Isabel. Any further conversation might lead to an accusation and such a move would be futile and, Isabel felt, dangerous. There was something threatening about this intense woman and Isabel wanted her out of her house. Also Pastry was snuffling around under her seat tugging at the knotted rope.

She was about to thank Margaret for calling, when there was an insistent rap on the front door.

Too late, thought Isabel. This had to be Perch. Isabel had no option but to tell him what she knew with Margaret Dunstan present. She could hardly boot her out the back door. Anyway, she felt Dunstan's suspicions were aroused. She heard Hattie answer the door and a man's voice said:

"Where is she?"

The next moment Sergeant Perch, red faced, strode angrily through the door unannounced and slammed it behind him. Pastry growled, but cowered away from the man. Isabel stood up.

"I am here Sergeant."

"Right, you're coming along with me."

Isabel raised her hand.

"Before you try to arrest me, please listen to what I have to say."

Perch scowled and pointed an accusing finger.

"If you're going to give me all that nonsense about the killer being a woman, you can think again."

Isabel saw Margaret Dunstan flinch. Now was the time.

"It is not nonsense," she replied, calmly. "I have to admit, contrary to your wishes, I visited Giles Chichester's flat." She looked at Margaret Dunstan. "Behind a cabinet with an enamelled door, I found a blood stained hand print. I believe the killer, covered in blood, tripped on their way out and steadied themselves on the wall. I believe they moved the cabinet to hide it."

Dunstan visibly blanched.

"What blood stained hand print?" growled Perch. "We found no such thing."

"It was concealed that's why," replied Isabel. She picked up the two photographs. "I saw the cabinet had been moved recently, due to the indentations in the carpet, and its position by the door didn't ring true. Here is the hand print with my hand beside it. You will see it is a small hand, obviously a woman's."

Perch squinted at the pictures.

"I don't follow you."

"I think if you compare the fingerprints on the wall of the flat, with those on this." She picked up the sherry glass and held it carefully by the stem. "You will find them one and the same. Isn't that so Miss Dunstan, as you know they are your fingerprints?" The woman didn't reply. "And I have to tell you also, Sergeant, that Miss Dunstan owns a white cat, which used to sleep in her father's cap. The same cap, I daresay, which the killer left in the road after the collision with the milk cart. And she has a badly bruised knee, where she was kicked by Fred Ames's horse, Nancy. Has it left an imprint of its shoe on your knee Miss Dunstan? Is that why you refused to see a doctor about it?"

Margaret, now ashen, saw she was cornered. She scowled.

"You've tricked me and my mother."

"Yes I have," said Isabel. "I'm sorry. But, I had no choice. I'm afraid it's over, Margaret."

Margaret didn't agree. She stood up and made a run for the door.

"Just one minute, young lady," said Perch, making to grab her arm. There was a sudden flash and Margaret pulled one of Isabel's kitchen knives from her pocket. Isabel gasped. She must have collected it on her way in and that knife might have been meant for her. Dunstan stabbed Perch in the arm. He cried out and fell backwards onto the floor and she ran to the door, but, outside in the hall, stood Hattie with Tom Barry and two uniformed constables. She wheeled round and headed back towards Isabel. She would take her hostage; get out of the house that way. But Isabel threw the knotted rope in her path, which Pastry tore after. Dunstan stumbled momentarily over the rope and the dog, but when she regained her balance she found herself staring down the barrel of a revolver.

"Put my knife down, please Margaret," said Isabel calmly. "This has gone far enough. Hattie, get the first aid box. The Sergeant is bleeding all over my carpet."

"This is a mad house," groaned Perch.

Dunstan put the knife down on the floor and just looked blankly at Isabel.

"I don't regret it," she hissed. "So don't judge me. He was a vile man."

"From what people have told me, I agree," replied Isabel. "But, unfortunately, that was no excuse to murder him."

"He was going to ruin me," snarled Dunstan. "He spied on me and then had this article he was going to write. He gloated about it. He was going to tell everyone about my being a lesbian."

"He did write it," replied Isabel. She held up the sheet of typed paper. Margaret's eyes widened. "And I've read it. It is spiteful and vindictive in the extreme. I doubt the magazine would have published it. And if they had, with Chichester's reputation for embroidering the truth, there is no reason to suggest anyone would believe it. Most people have never heard the word lesbian and, if they have, don't know what it means. It is not illegal."

"Jen-Eva would have believed it," said Dunstan dully, "She believed everything he said. And, anyway, it's true, so I could never have denied it and lied to her. She despised lesbians you see. She said they were a threat to the union. I would have lost her, lost everything. I couldn't bear that. That's all he wanted, to have her all to himself. He didn't love her. Not like I did." She paused. "So I had to kill him."

There was a chilling edge to her voice.

Isabel nodded. This woman was on the edge she felt certain.

"Where is the knife?" she asked.

"Back in the drawer at Jen-Eva's. I washed it clean and returned it the next day. No one noticed."

"And the clothes you wore?"

"I burned them."

Tom Barry walked quietly into the sitting room.

"Miss Dunstan, come along with me. We need to discuss this further at the police station."

"No handcuffs, please," said Isabel, wanting to save the woman the indignity of that in the street. "I'm sure Miss Dunstan will behave herself."

They led her away without a word.

Meanwhile Hattie returned with the first aid box. She helped Sergeant Perch into a chair and removed his jacket and rolled up his sleeve.

"Just a flesh wound, Ma'am," she said to Isabel. She began to clean the cut.

"I'll get you a brandy," said Isabel. "Actually I think we could all do with one."

Then she remembered she was driving the ambulance that afternoon.

Better not, she thought, but still gave a large one to the Sergeant.

"What put you onto her?" asked Perch, trying hard not to groan. Hattie was too clumsy to make a good nurse. "When did you know it was her?"

"I didn't until this morning," replied Isabel. "I'm afraid it was her mother, who gave her away."

Tom Barry returned to collect what evidence Isabel had. He took the sherry glass, the kitchen knife and the photographs, but Isabel withheld the article. She didn't want the whole of Scotland Yard sniggering about Miss Dunstan. And the woman had confessed to the murder, so it wasn't required. Perhaps, too, she felt a loyalty to Elvira and those secret patrons of the Golden Lion.

Two constables also helped Sergeant Perch out to an awaiting police car. He grunted an acknowledgement to Isabel, which, she assumed, was the only thanks she would get. Pastry, who had been rather excited by all the action, had finished chewing the knotted rope and was asleep again in the shaft of sunlight.

Mrs Rhodes, though, was outraged.

"She chose my sharpest one," she declared, "the little madam coming in the back way whilst my back was turned!"

"I'll get a replacement," reassured Isabel. She didn't like the thought of that one being used in her kitchen again either. Then she caught sight of the time. She would have to leave soon. She hurried upstairs to get changed into her uniform.

EPILOGUE

When Isabel returned from driving the ambulance, Mrs Rhodes had a message for her.

"Miss Howard called. She wants to speak to you. I told her to call back at 4."

Which is any time soon, thought Isabel. She had told Clarke the drama of the morning and he was to join her at home, later.

"Would you care for tea, Ma'am?" asked Mrs Rhodes.

"That would be most welcome," replied Isabel.

She went into the sitting room to make the customary extravagant fuss of Pastry, who behaved as if she hadn't seen her mistress for days. On the carpet by the door was a wet patch. Mrs Rhodes had done an admirable job in wiping up Sergeant Perch's blood. He had been taken to hospital and his wound stitched. Margaret Dunstan was being held in the cells at a local police station. She had been charged with murder.

Isabel gathered that Inspector Mangle had taken over the case, so all the right procedures would be followed. Margaret had been examined by a doctor and her knee was found to be still badly bruised and there was a fading outline of a horse shoe. But, now she was getting proper medical treatment. Mangle had even been to Chichester's flat and viewed the blood stained handprint. Samples had been taken. The identity of Perch's burglar was still a mystery. Isabel just hoped it wasn't Reggie Biddle.

She had hardly time to sit down and drink her tea, when there was a knock on the front door. Moments later, Hattie showed Jen-Eva Howard into the room.

"Miss Hewitt," she began going on the offensive immediately, "what is all this nonsense about Margaret being arrested for murdering dear Giles?"

"Sadly because it is true," replied Isabel, not standing up. "She has confessed. And, sad to say, there is evidence to prove it."

Her visitor was astounded. Isabel indicated a seat and Jen-Eva sat down.

"But, but I don't understand. I thought Giles disturbed a burglar. Why on earth would Margaret want to harm Giles?"

"Because he wanted to harm her," replied Isabel. "He planned to publish a scurrilous article about her in that magazine of his, which would have seriously damaged her reputation and, I daresay, her relationship with you."

Jen-Eva's brown corrugated.

"With me? How?"

Isabel saw no point in hiding the truth, although she didn't want Jen-Eva seeing the article.

"Are you aware that your secretary is a lesbian?"

Jen-Eva looked at her in amazement.

"Is that what all this is about?"

Isabel nodded.

"So, you did know."

"Let's just say I suspected it, Miss Hewitt. She has a room in my house with a wardrobe for her clothes, if she needs to change for meetings. I had occasion to look in there once and found a well-tailored man's suit. It could only have been hers due to the size. But I valued Margaret too much to let that bother me. What she did in her own time was her business, provided she was discreet and didn't discredit the union, which she didn't."

"She thinks you despise lesbians and, consequently, would despise her if you found out, that you would terminate her employment with you."

"I wouldn't have done that, Miss Hewitt. Anyway I only despise those loud lesbians, who try and influence others to their way of thinking. Margaret never did that. I would never sack *her*. She knew me better than that."

"She didn't know you better than that, Miss Howard. In fact she said she was desperate not to lose you. You see, I suspect she is in love with you."

Jen-Eva's hand flew to her mouth.

"What? I didn't realise *that*. I didn't know she had those sort of feelings for me. When Giles…" she stopped abruptly.

Isabel gave Jen-Eva a level glance.

"When Giles… what? Did you discuss it with him? Did you tell him about the suit?"

Jen-Eva looked uneasy.

"We'd had too much champagne. He made a comment about he thought Margaret was a lesbian and I said it wouldn't surprise me, what with the suit in the wardrobe. It was just a casual remark. I didn't think anything of it. I thought he was joking."

Isabel frowned. This stupid woman had played right into Chichester's hands and, unwittingly, betrayed her friend.

"No. He was deadly serious, Miss Howard. He began spying on her with a view to exposing her in that rag of his. He followed her to Soho, where there is a private club for lesbians."

"But why? She'd never done him any harm."

Isabel shrugged.

"I assume he wanted her out of the way. And I gather he liked to control people. And he disapproved of her influence over you. A colleague at the magazine told me that."

"Yes, yes." Miss Howard was dismissive. "But I knew how to manage him. Are you sure he spied on her."

"Yes, Miss Howard. I'm afraid your late fiancé had a very cruel streak."

Miss Howard protested.

"He was always charming and loving with me and popular with all my friends. I just can't believe Giles could be cruel to anyone."

Isabel sighed.

"Well, charming or not, Miss Howard, he was cruel to Margaret. He pushed her too far, so she killed him. She stabbed him 27 times, as proof of the great distress she felt."

Jen-Eva just looked at Isabel in horror.

"Oh, Margaret, what have I done? And all because Giles…" She put her head in her hands, as a maelstrom of guilt and regret gripped her. Isabel politely said nothing. Presently Jen-Eva looked up. "What will happen to her?"

"She will be tried for murder I expect and, if found guilty…"

"But, surely it was a crime of passion. Margaret is not a violent person. She must have lost her reason. This is totally out of character. She's a pacifist."

"That might be a defence, but, I'm afraid, the fact she disguised herself and lay in wait for Giles indicates premeditation. Only a lawyer can advise on that."

Jen-Eva looked round, desperately trying to think of some way to help.

"What can I do? I must do something for her."

"Go and see her. Tell her you know the truth and don't despise her for being a lesbian. She loves you, whether or not you can return the love. She needs your support now." Isabel paused. "And hire a good lawyer for her. If Margaret behaved out of character, and had temporarily lost her reason, it may help. Having spoken to her this morning, I suspect that may be true. But I am not a doctor. I cannot say for sure."

Jen-Eva nodded. Isabel could see she was close to tears.

"My family have a very good lawyer. I will contact him immediately. Where is Margaret being held?"

"Ring Scotland Yard and ask for Inspector Mangle. He will advise you."

Jen-Eva stood up.

"Oh, and I must pay you."

"I will send you my bill," said Isabel. "I'm sorry that this regrettable business has had such an unfavourable outcome."

Jen-Eva nodded.

"So am I Miss Hewitt. So am I. I will go and see Margaret's family, too. They need a full explanation from me. The guilt lies at my door. I had no idea that a flippant remark from me would prompt Giles to do this to her."

"I don't think they know Margaret's secret," warned Isabel.

"Then I won't tell them," replied Jen-Eva.

"One more thing," said Isabel. "I'm afraid Margaret used one of your kitchen knives to stab Giles. Only she can tell you which one. The police will want it, even though she cleaned it."

This was the last straw. Jen-Eva hurried away to see Dunstan's parents.

And I must avoid Tavistock Place for a while thought Isabel. I doubt Mrs Dunstan would be pleased to see me.

Later Clarke arrived back at Cartwright Gardens. Pastry barked more than normal, when she heard his voice. He opened the sitting room door. A grey, hairy dog's head with a long snout peered around the door frame. Pastry sped across the room and skidded to a halt as the dog stepped inside.

"Tucker I presume," said Isabel, standing up and smiling.

Clarke nodded.

"Yes, here he is. You said you wanted to meet him."

"Indeed I did."

He led the dog into the room.

"He's very well behaved and, don't worry. He doesn't have fleas, not anymore."

Pastry's big eyes looked up at the new dog, and then her curly tail wagged. Tucker's tail swished as he sniffed the little pug.

"They like each other," said Clarke.

Isabel laughed and walked over to stroke the lurcher.

"Good. Hello Tucker, welcome to Cartwright Gardens. You must come and live with us."

Until you and Clarke have to go away again, she thought, but didn't say so. She planned to make the most of every day she had left with them both.

And, at least for the time being, there would be two dogs to chase Sapphire, the white cat, in the gardens.

THE END

Miss Hewitt Investigates the White Cat